BUSHWHACKED

"You should learn how to move through brush, Coles," Decker said. "You picked the one place to meet me in this city where you'd be at a disadvantage instead of me."

"You son of a bitch," Coles said. "You challenged me."

"And you lost," Decker said. He pressed the shotgun into the small of Coles's back and said, "Just stand still." He patted the man down and removed a Colt .45 from a shoulder rig . . . He stepped forward and brought the butt of the .45 down hard on the point of Coles's shoulder.

Decker grabbed Coles's left wrist, twisted it behind him and brought the .45 down on it hard. The sound of the arm breaking was sharp and loud, and Coles screamed.

"Where's the girl?"

"Jesus, my elbow—"

Decker grabbed the arm and pulled it back. Coles screamed again. "You've got one broken arm, Coles," Decker said. "You want to try for two?"

"I don't know—"

Decker put the .45 next to Coles's left ear and fired it. Coles screamed.

"Jesus, I'm deaf!"

"OK," Decker said, "you got a broken arm, a bad left knee, and you're deaf in your left ear." He grabbed Coles's right arm, pulled it straight back and said, "Let's start on the right side."

ROBERT J. RANDISI

Broadway Bounty

LEISURE BOOKS NEW YORK CITY

A LEISURE BOOK®

August 2010

Published by

Dorchester Publishing Co., Inc.
200 Madison Avenue
New York, NY 10016

ISBN 10: 0-8439-6432-5
ISBN 13: 978-0-8439-6432-5
E-ISBN: 978-1-4285-0913-9

Visit us online at www.dorchesterpub.com.

Broadway Bounty

Prologue

Decker turned the body over to look at the face. He already knew what he would see, but when the face came into view, he flinched, anyway.

Once Dover and Decker had been friends. That had been a long time ago, when they were younger—Jesus, when they were kids. People had commented on the similarity of their names—Dover and Decker—as if that made them brothers.

Then one day they went their separate ways. Decker ended up a bounty hunter.

So did Dover.

Now, more than fifteen years later, Dover was cold meat.

Decker let Dover's body go, and it flopped onto its stomach again. The three gunshot wounds in his back had been cleaned and were now just pink, puckered holes. Decker felt cold, but not as cold as Dover.

"Who did it?" he asked the undertaker.

"You'll have to ask the sheriff that."

"You don't know?"

"Why would I know?" the undertaker said. "That doesn't matter to me. The who, the why, the where, none of that matters to me."

"No," Decker said, "I don't guess it does."

"Passing judgment on me, bounty hunter? You kill 'em, and I plant 'em. Which one of us is worse?"

"I don't pass judgment," Decker said. He headed for the door.

"I guess he was a friend of yours."

Decker stopped and turned around.

"He was."

"So then I guess you'd know if he had any kin?"

"He didn't."

"The sheriff has his personal stuff," the undertaker said. "Don't let him tell you different."

Decker stood there for a few seconds. Then he said, "Thanks. I'll be paying for his burial."

"Anything special?"

"No, nothing special."

"Come back after you talk to the sheriff, and we'll settle up."

Decker nodded and left.

"Sheriff?"

The sheriff of Harrison City, Iowa, looked up from behind his desk.

"Did you see your friend?"

"I did."

"Nice, neat job."

Decker gave the man a hard stare.

"Who did it?"

"How come you just happen to ride in the day it happened?"

"I was supposed to meet him today."

"Got here a little late, didn't you?"

"No," Decker said, "I got here just in time."

The lawman raised his eyebrows but said nothing.

"Who did it?"

"The Tyrone brothers."

"Why?"

"You'll have to ask them."

"How many of them?"

"Three," the sheriff said, "one for each hole."

"Why aren't they in jail?"

"Because, Decker," the sheriff said, "there are three of them and one of me. I'm not a fool."

"Where are they?"

"The saloon, I guess."

Decker hesitated a moment, then said, "When I've finished with them, I'll be back to talk to you."

The look on the lawman's face said he doubted that very much.

Decker turned and left.

Decker stopped right outside the only saloon in Harrison City and looked around. Apparently the shooting incident had driven many of the townspeople inside, for the streets were virtually empty.

Maybe they knew it wasn't over yet.

Decker squared his shoulders and went into the saloon. There was only one man there, sitting at a table with a beer. Decker walked to the bar and ordered a whiskey. When the bartender put it in front of him, Decker put the money on the bar. As the man went to take it, he caught his wrist.

In a low voice he said, "The Tyrone brothers."

When the man saw the look in Decker's eyes, any thoughts he had of not answering immediately fled.

"That's one of them over there," he said. "That there's Virgil."

"And the other two?"

"Up-upstairs."

"Good," Decker said. "Now disappear."

"Y-yessir."

Decker downed the whiskey, and as it burned its way down his throat, he turned and faced Virgil Tyrone.

"Tyrone?"

The man looked up. He had the biggest ears Decker had ever seen.

"Who are you?"

"Decker."

"I don't know you."

"But I know you. You killed a friend of mine."

"Yeah? Who?"

"Dover."

"Oh, yeah. The bounty hunter."

"That's right."

"And you? Are you a bounty hunter?"

"Yes."

"And now you wanna *kill* me?"

"I don't have a choice," Decker said. "This town doesn't have any law to speak of."

"Yeah, I've noticed that myself," Tyrone said. "You know there are two more of us, don't you?"

"Yes."

"Do you intend to kill them, too?"

"Yes."

"Well," Tyrone said, standing, "I guess you'll have to start somewhere."

The man was a fool. While he was spreading his legs and readying himself for a fair draw, Decker pulled his sawed-off shotgun and killed him.

"Shit," Decker said. "If I fought fair, I'd have been dead long ago."

Decker went up the steps slowly, reloading his gun. He had no way of knowing if the bartender had told the truth, but he played it as if he had—figuring the other two Tyrone brothers were upstairs, doing what men did upstairs in a saloon.

On the second floor he paused to listen. What he heard gave him the impression that two men were having a good time.

He started down the hall, moving cautiously, on the lookout for creaking floorboards—not that any- one would have heard him. By this time a man was moaning loudly and a woman was making a high- pitched, keening sound. One of the brothers was real close to finishing his good time.

Decker found the door where most of the noise was coming from. He held his gun in his right hand and braced himself against the wall opposite the door with his left. He pushed off and kicked out at the door, hitting it right next to the doorknob with his heel. The door splintered and slammed open.

On the bed he could see a man's naked ass and a woman's legs. The man turned and stared at him, open-mouthed, and a girl leaned sideways to take a look.

"What the—" the man said. He pushed himself off the girl and onto his back. "Who are you?"

"The question is, who are you?" Decker said. The question was unnecessary because the family re- semblance was striking—especially around the ears.

"Matt Tyrone."

"My name's Decker," Decker said. "Dover was my friend."

"Dover?"

"The man you and your brothers killed about two hours ago."

Virgil looked at the sawed-off in Decker's hand and licked his lips.

"You can't shoot me while I'm unarmed."

"There's your gun," Decker said, gesturing toward the gun belt hanging on the bedpost.

At that moment a man's voice from behind Decker said, "Jesus, Matt, what're you doin' to the bitch? It sounds like—"

When he saw Decker, the man quickly backed out and ran down the hall. No doubt he was after his gun.

The man on the bed took the opportunity to move for his own gun, knocking the woman off the bed as he did. As it turned out, he knocked her out of the line of Decker's fire.

As Matt Tyrone's hand closed over the butt of his gun, Decker fired, catching the man in the back of the head and blowing it apart.

The woman—who was forty if she was a day—started to scream. Blood had splattered her naked body.

Decker put his back to the wall and quickly reloaded. The third Tyrone brother had his gun by now, and he was either gone or waiting in the hall.

The woman on the floor was still screaming, and Decker shouted, "Shut up!" Shocked, she fell silent, except for an occasional sob.

Quickly he moved past the woman to look out the window. It was a sheer drop to the street below, no ledge, no balcony. He moved back over to the wall next to the door and listened intently.

"Mike, what the hell is—" called a woman.

She was talking to Mike Tyrone. "Jesus," Tyrone yelled, "Shut up! Get back inside!"

Both voices came from the hallway.

Decker moved away from the wall and jumped out into the hallway, keeping low.

Mike Tyrone was square in the center of the hall with his gun out. He'd just pushed someone into his room, and when he looked back down the hall, Decker was there. Tyrone—there were those family ears again—brought his gun up, but Decker pulled the triggers on his shotgun and splattered him all over the hallway.

"I told you I'd be back."

The sheriff looked up from his desk and stared at Decker for a long moment.

"Heard some shooting," he finally said. "The Tyrone boys dead?"

"Yep."

"All three, huh? You're good."

"The best," Decker said, moving toward the desk. "Now it's your turn." The sheriff looked as if he might reach for his gun.

"You make a move for that gun and this town's going to need a new sheriff."

"What do you want?" the sheriff asked warily.

"Is there paper on the Tyrone boys?"

"No."

"Then why did they kill Dover?"

"The only reason those boys did anything is because someone told them to."

"Who?"

"I don't know."

"Sheriff—"

"I really don't know," the lawman said. "Dover had a room at the hotel. Maybe you'll find something there."

Decker shook his head and said, "How did you get that badge, anyway—by default?"

"How'd you know that?"

"Lucky guess. By the way, I want Dover's personal effects."

"I-I don't have them," the sheriff said. "Ask the undertaker."

Decker leaned on the desk and said, "I'm asking you."

Decker went to the hotel and got Dover's hotel key from the clerk. In Dover's room he looked around but found nothing but some extra shirts, an extra gun and some bullets.

He sat on the bed and looked at the stuff he'd gotten from the sheriff. Some money in a wallet—there had probably been more, which the sheriff had spent—a letter to someone named Jane which Dover hadn't mailed yet, and an old knife, which Decker recognized. Dover'd had that knife a long time, and the blade had dulled over the years. He'd only kept it as a lucky piece.

He dropped the knife and picked up the wallet from the bed. He riffled through it and found a folded-up paper. He unfolded it and spread it out. It was a poster on a man named Oakley Ready. Decker had never heard of him, but the price was high, five thousand. He was wanted for three murders.

He was wanted by Decker for a fourth. The only reason Dover would have hidden the poster was he didn't want anyone else to see it. He wanted to make sure he got this man himself.

"I'll get him for you, Dover."

As Decker refolded the poster, he saw some writing on the back—a list of cities. It was probably the route over which Dover had tracked Ready.

There were two cities left on the list. One was Harrison City. Dover had died here. The other city on the list was probably where Dover expected to find Oakley Ready.

When Decker left the hotel carrying his gear, the Tyrone boys had been removed. He stopped at the sheriff's office on his way to the livery.

"You clean up real quick," he said to the sheriff.

"Yeah," the sheriff said. He was pouring himself a cup of coffee and didn't offer Decker one.

"I guess you're the town garbage man, too, huh?"

The sheriff opened his mouth to reply, then thought better of it. He knew Decker's reputation.

"Did you check out the Tyrone boys?" Decker asked.

"Uh, what do you mean . . . check them out?"

"Don't play dense with me, Sheriff," Decker said. "How much money did they have on them?"

"Uh, they each had more than one hundred dollars on them."

"One hundred dollars?" Decker asked. "Are they local?"

"Yeah."

"How long would it take them to earn that kind of money in this town?"

The sheriff laughed and said, "In a week, a month or a year?"

"Where's the money now?"

Very quickly the sheriff's eyes went to his desk, and then away.

"I . . . guess it's at the undertaker's—"

Decker walked around behind the desk and started opening drawers.

"Hey, you can't do that—"

"You gonna stop me?" Decker asked.

The sheriff took one step forward, then stopped and took two steps back, shaking his head in disgust.

Decker found the money in a drawer and took it out. There was more than five hundred dollars there. He counted out enough for four burials and dropped it on the desk.

"I'll be back to see the graves," he said.

The sheriff hesitated a moment. Then he licked his lips and said, "They'll be there."

He watched as Decker tucked the rest of the money into his pocket and walked out.

Decker went to the livery, retrieved his horse and rode out of town. He had to find the nearest railroad and start his journey to New York City.

Chapter One

During the train trip to New York, Decker thought a lot about Dover . . .

. . . about a conversation they'd had when they were both seventeen.

"I wanna be the best lawman I can be," Dover said. "I wanna be famous."

"You want to be rich, too?" Decker had asked.

Dover had smiled.

"If that comes with it, fine."

"A lot of other things come with being famous, Dove," Decker had warned him.

"Good things."

"Bad things, too."

"Like what?" the youthful Dover had asked.

"Like people trying to kill you."

Dover had laughed, filled with bravado, and said, "Never happen . . ."

Well, Dover had achieved a certain degree of fame, and now he *was* dead.

And then there was that incident that happened when they were both twenty, when they became deputies, against Decker's better judgment . . .

. . . they were passing through an Arizona town, stopping to sample the whiskey and other pleasures that a small town like that might have to offer. In the saloon they heard shooting in the street and rushed to the door with the other patrons. The bank was being robbed.

In front of the bank was a man holding five skittish horses. Four other men came piling out, each carrying a bag filled with money. Apparently the robbery had not gone smoothly and some shooting had been done inside the bank.

This had alerted the local law, and the sheriff and two deputies came running onto the scene, guns drawn. After a brief exchange the five bank robbers rode out and the sheriff's two deputies lay dead in the street.

When the shooting had stopped, people began to file out onto the street. The sheriff asked for volunteers to carry the body of his two deputies off the street, and he got them.

Then he asked for volunteers for a posse to follow the bank robbers and track them . . . and he got none.

Dover stepped forward, pulling Decker along with him.

"We'll volunteer," he said.

We, Decker thought.

The sheriff said, "You boys are strangers in town. Why volunteer?"

Dover shrugged. "So? Why look a gift horse in the mouth?"

The sheriff stared at him.

"You've got a point there," he said.

Then he bent down and took the deputy badges off his dead men and handed them to Dover and Decker.

"We'll worry about the swearing-in later," he said. "Get your horses."

As they went to the livery for their horses, Decker

said, "What the hell was that all about? Didn't anybody ever tell you it's not healthy to volunteer for anything?"

"Hell," Dover said, "do we have anything better to do?"

"I've always got something better to do than die," Decker said.

On the train, Decker studied the poster of Oakley Ready.

He wondered why Dover had sent him a message to meet him in Harrison City. Had he known that he was going to need help with this Ready character? In spite of their friendship, their paths didn't cross more than two or three times a year, and they had never worked together or split a bounty. Dover must have asked Decker for help because he knew that Ready was going to be especially tough to take.

That bothered Decker.

Dover was one of the toughest men he'd ever known, and he'd been taken the only way a man like him could be taken—from behind!

And that was the real reason Decker was in New York—the fact that Dover had been shot in the back!

The Tyrone brothers had pulled the trigger, but the odds were that Oakley Ready had paid them to do it.

As the train pulled into the station, Decker put the poster away and grabbed his bag. The trip had been planned—if that word could be used—on the spur of the moment, and he didn't have much in the way of gear with him. He had his gun, his rifle and some extra clothes, and that was all.

As a conductor went by, Decker stopped him for a moment.

"How do I get to a hotel from the station?"

"You can take the horsecars, sir, or a private cab. The horsecars are cheaper."

"Thank you."

As the train began to discharge passengers at the station, Decker found himself in the middle of a pressing crowd. He'd never seen so many people in one place at one time before, trying to fit into the same space.

Being jostled did not sit well with him, so he broke free as soon as he could.

He spotted the horsecars immediately. They looked like railroad cars being pulled by horses.

"Need a cab, sir?" a voice asked.

He turned and saw a man standing nearby.

"What?"

"A ride?" the man said. "Do you need a ride somewhere?"

"Well, I was thinking of taking the horsecar—" Decker said, pointing.

"You don't want to do that, sir," the young man said.

"Why?"

The man made a face.

"You'll save money, but they're filthy, badly ventilated and full of vermin—some of it walking around on two legs, if you know what I mean."

"You paint a fine picture."

"Now, if you take my cab, it's clean, and private."

"And expensive?"

"Some people might think so," the man said, "but since you just got to town, I'll make you a special rate. What do you say?"

"Yeah, sure," Decker said. "Why not?"

"This way."

He followed the man to a horse-drawn cab, similar to ones he had once seen in Washington, D.C.

"Get in."

Decker hesitated.

"You're from the West, aren't you?" the man asked. He was young, in his twenties, and very slim, with a shock of unkempt brown hair.

"Good guess."

"You're gonna need some clothes."

"Clothes?"

"Unless you want to attract attention every time you walk down the street."

"Do you know where I can get some?"

"Sure."

"Cheap?"

"Well . . . let's say inexpensive."

"And then a hotel to match?"

"I know just the place," the driver said.

"All right," Decker said, "let's go."

Using the money generously donated by the Tyrone boys—Oakley Ready's money—Decker bought himself two suits of clothes suitable for New York.

"Here's the hotel."

"It doesn't look inexpensive."

"I could take you to a hotel that could fit this one in the lobby."

Decker looked out at the huge brick structure on Twenty-third Street, then back at the driver.

"OK," he said, getting out of the cab. He grabbed his bag and his rifle and looked at the driver.

"You're gonna need a gun," the driver said.

"What makes you say that?"

The man smiled.

"You gonna wear those clothes with that gun on your hip?"

Decker looked down at the sawed-off shotgun in his holster and nodded.

"I see what you mean."

"I can get you a gun."

"A decent one?"

"Hell, a good one."

"Yeah? How much?"

The man thought a moment.

"I'll tell you what," he said finally. "A hundred dollars. The ride, the gun, everything."

Decker studied the man's eyes.

"If I give you a hundred dollars—"

"Don't worry," the man said. "My name's Billy Rosewood. Ask anybody in New York. I'm reliable."

"Reliable," Decker said.

Rosewood nodded.

Decker took out Dover's lucky knife and asked, "Will you get this sharpened for me, too?"

Rosewood grinned and took it.

"Sure, no extra charge."

"OK," Decker said. He gave Billy Rosewood a hundred dollars, knowing he might be kissing it goodbye.

What the hell—

It wasn't his money, anyway.

Chapter Two

Decker found the room rate prohibitive, but he checked into the hotel anyway. At the rate that he was spending the money he got from the Tyrone brothers, it wouldn't be long before he was broke.

When he saw the room, he found it almost worth the price. It was more lavish than any other room he'd ever had, save the one his friend Duke Ballard had given him when he went to San Francisco.

There were even a bathtub, which he made use of immediately. When he was drying himself, there was a knock on the door. He wrapped a towel around his waist and answered it.

It was Billy Rosewood.

"That was fast," Decker said.

"I know where to get things in this town," Billy assured him.

"Come on in."

Rosewood entered, and Decker closed the door.

"Hey," Rosewood said, taking a good look at Decker, "were you ever a boxer?"

"No."

"You look like you could've been . . . although those don't look like boxing scars."

Glancing at the scars on his torso, Decker said, "They're not. What have you got for me?"

"Ah—here."

Rosewood took out a leather shoulder rig with a gun in the holster from inside his jacket. He removed the gun and showed it to Decker.

"It's a Colt New Line," Rosewood said. "Thirty-two caliber. That was the biggest caliber I could find in a gun this small."

Decker took the gun and held it.

"It holds five shots," Rosewood said. "I can get you a twenty-two-caliber gun that holds seven shots if you like."

"No, this is fine," Decker said. "If five shots doesn't do it, I don't think two extra will matter."

Decker checked to see that the gun was fully loaded, then put it down on the dresser.

"Here," Rosewood said, handing him the shoulder rig, "no extra charge."

"I'm touched by your generosity, Billy," Decker said, accepting it.

"I'm not so generous really. I figure if you're gonna be here awhile, I might get some repeat business."

"Well, I will need someone to show me around."

"I'm your man. You know how to put that thing on?" he asked, indicating the shoulder holster.

"I'll figure it out."

"Anything I can do for you now?"

"Not today," Decker said. "I'm going to walk around a bit, find a telegraph office and a decent restaurant."

"Well, don't eat in the hotel dining room. There's a restaurant two blocks west that makes a pretty good steak dinner."

"Thanks."

"Three blocks to the east and then a block north, you'll find a telegraph office."

"Well," Decker said, "that's all I need for now."

"If you had more money to spend and were staying in a better hotel, there'd be a telegraph line right in the hotel itself."

"I'll remember that next time I'm here. Can you meet me out front at nine in the morning?"

"Nine sharp," Rosewood said. "I'll be there."

"See you then. I'll buy you breakfast."

"You got a deal." Rosewood started for the door. "Oh, I almost forgot."

He took Dover's lucky knife from his belt.

"Got you a real nice edge on this," he said, handing it to Decker. "Why'd you let it get so dull?"

"It belonged to a friend of mine. He carried it only for luck."

"I presume he's dead?"

"Yes."

"Well, with an edge like that on it, you should have more luck with it than he did."

"I hope so."

"See you in the morning."

"Right."

Rosewood left, and Decker got dressed. He slipped on the shoulder holster and then slid the gun into it. It was uncomfortable, but he'd get used to it. His only worry was that he was not a good marksman with a pistol, and the gun was only a .32. With the small caliber, it would have been better if he could hit what he wanted when he wanted, but this would have to do.

He put on one of the suits he'd just bought and

checked himself in the mirror. The gun was nestled beneath his arm and hardly showed at all. It would take a tailor's expert eye to catch it.

Satisfied, he left the room to take a little get-acquainted-with-New-York walk.

Chapter Three

Decker didn't think he could ever live in New York. The streets and sidewalks were too hard on a man's feet, and he was damn sure that the streets were too hard on a horse's hoof, too. He was glad he'd left John Henry with a friend in St. Louis, the farthest east he'd ever been before this trip.

He found the restaurant Billy Rosewood told him about and ordered the steak dinner. It came with potatoes, onions, two other vegetables and biscuits. He had two cold beers with it, and it all went down fine. Not like Western cooking, but fine.

He walked the other way then and found the telegraph office where Billy Rosewood said it would be, on Fifth Avenue and Twenty-fifth Street.

Inside, he composed a message to his friend Duke, in San Francisco. He wanted to know if Duke knew who Oakley Ready was and what he might be doing in New York. If not, he asked if Duke knew anyone in New York that could give him the answers.

"If I get an answer, can you have someone run it over to my hotel?" he asked, handing the clerk some money.

"Sure thing, mister."

"Thanks." He started to leave, then turned back and asked, "Is there any place nearby I could get a drink?"

"A couple of places, but try the bar across the

street, near Twenty-sixth. Better atmosphere." The clerk wriggled his eyebrows.

"Thanks again."

"Enjoy yourself."

Decker went over to Twenty-sixth and entered the bar.

"Yes, sir?" asked a fat bartender. "What can I get for you?"

"A cold beer."

"Only kind we serve, sir."

"Fine."

Decker looked around, wondering why anyone would put so much money into making a bar look so grand. The seats were cushioned and leather covered, and there were chandeliers made of metal and glass—and this was just a street bar, where somebody would stop for a drink after work, or something?

It was barely dark out, and the place was only half full. There were a few girls working the place, and they were as dressed up as the bar. All three of them were under twenty-five and pretty. If Decker were interested, he would have picked the dark-haired girl over the two blondes, but that was not what he was here in New York for.

He finished his beer and walked back to his hotel.

Decker tensed, not sure what had wakened him. He kept perfectly still, listening intently. The shoulder rig with the New Line was hanging on the bedpost, but his shotgun was close by, within reach on a small night table.

He listened for a few moments and finally heard it again, a scratching noise at the door.

Somebody was trying to get in.

He leaped off the bed. Grabbing the shotgun, he stood next to the door, so that he'd be behind it when it opened.

Whoever it was didn't have a whole lot of experience. It took him a few more minutes to get it done finally.

Once it was unlocked, the door swung open slowly until Decker was standing right behind it. He raised the shotgun in his right hand and waited for the man to enter. In the light coming from the hall, he could see that his bed was empty. If he could see it, so could whoever had just opened his door.

He hit the door hard with his shoulder and felt it bang into someone. Coming around the door fast, he found he'd made a mistake.

There were two of them.

One of them was sitting in the hall with a bloody nose; the other one stepped into Decker's path and returned the favor. He was a big man, and with one hand he grabbed the barrel of the shotgun. With the other he hit Decker in the face with a massive fist. Decker backpedaled quickly, trying to keep his balance, and finally went down at the foot of the bed.

His nose was bleeding, and his eyes were tearing. He felt he deserved it, for being so careless. He'd allowed the fact that he was in a strangae town, where nobody should know him, to lull him into a false sense of security.

The big man picked his partner up from the hall and pushed him into the room, then entered behind him. He turned up the lamp by the door and then faced Decker, holding his shotgun.

"Get up," the big man said.

Decker stood up, wiping the blood from the lower portion of his face with the back of his hand.

"Sit on the bed."

Decker started around the bed in the direction of his new .32, but the big man stopped him.

"Not that way!"

Decker turned and looked at him. He was well over six feet, with wide shoulders and huge hands, one of which was pointing Decker's own shotgun at him.

"That way," the big man said.

Decker went around the other side and sat down by the pillow.

"Get the other gun," the big man told his partner, whose face was also covered with blood.

"Let me kill him," the second man said. He was shorter, a slender man whose nose had been like a hawk's—once.

"Just get the gun, stupid."

"Don't call me stupid," the second man said sullenly.

"You said you could open the door," the big man complained.

"I opened it, didn't I?" the second man said, removing the .32 and shoulder rig from the bedpost.

"Yeah, it took you all night and you woke the whole hotel doing it."

"You guys want something," Decker said, "or are you going to argue me to death?"

"Funny man," the big man said.

Decker took hold of the sheet with one hand and used it to wipe the blood from his face. His nose had stopped bleeding. Unlike the second man's, his nose wasn't broken.

"What did you do? Follow me from the train station?"

"That's right."

Another mistake. Dover had been on Ready's trail for a long time. It made sense that Ready would have the station covered just in case he showed up.

Decker wondered if these two thought he was Dover because of his Western clothes and style.

"What do you want?"

"You," the big man said.

Decker looked at the second man. He was standing there holding the shoulder rig in his hand. He hadn't taken the gun out of the holster.

"Why me?"

"Because you're the guy," the big man said.

"I am?" Decker asked, putting his hand underneath the pillow.

"Yeah, you're him," the big man said, walking around to face Decker. The shotgun was pointing in his general direction.

"You fellas want to tell me what you want, or do you want me to kick you out of here?"

The second man laughed.

"Hey, Boil," he said, "you hear that? He's gonna kick you out of here."

"How do you intend to do that, Dover?" the big man—Boil—asked. "We have your guns."

"What'd you call me?"

"Dover."

"You've got the wrong man, friend," Decker said. "My name isn't Dover."

"Uh-huh," Boil said. "And you didn't get off the train today wearing Western clothes and looking like you just came in off the farm."

"Is that it?" Decker said. "You don't like farmers. I thought it was something personal."

"Stop fooling around, Boil," the second man said. "Let's kill him and get out." His hand was on the butt of the .32. Decker had to make a move before he palmed it.

"All right," Boil said. "I guess the fun is over." As he said this, he spread his hands, so that the shotgun pointed toward the wall for a split second.

Decker pulled Dover's sharpened knife out from under the pillow and lunged forward, burying it in Boil's stomach.

Boil screamed. Decker grabbed the shotgun from his hand and rolled on the floor a few feet, coming to a stop on his knees. The second man had already pulled the .32 from the holster and was pointing it at Decker. They pulled their respective triggers at the same time.

A .32 slug punched its way into Decker's left shoulder as his blast took the second man in the belly, ripping him apart and throwing him back against the wall.

Decker stood up and checked both men to make sure they were dead. Then and only then did he check his own wound.

"Jesus," he said, "I'm lucky I didn't buy a Colt .45 from Rosewood."

Chapter Four

"I think you're going to need a new room, Mr. Decker."

Decker looked up from the bed where he was sitting, holding a wadded-up pillow case against his wound. The man speaking had introduced himself as Lieutenant Tally of the New York City police department.

"This one's kind of messed up."

He looked over at the wall that Decker's shot had thrown the second man against. The wall was smeared with blood, and the man was still lying against the base of it.

"Do you know these two?" Decker asked.

The first man had already been carried out, and now two men entered to carry the second man out.

"The gun near him is mine," Decker said. "I'd like it back. Also the knife."

"You'll get them," Tally said. "To answer your question, yeah, I do know them. For a dollar and a half they'd kill their own mother. As a matter of fact, they did."

"They were brothers?"

"Yes. One was called Boil, the other Clyde."

"I see."

"Would you mind telling me what they wanted?"

"They said they wanted me."

"What for?"

"They said they were going to kill me."

"What for?"

"They didn't say that."

"What did they say?"

"That they followed me from the train station."

"They say why?"

"To kill me."

"Are we back to that again?"

"I'm afraid so."

"And you don't know why?"

"No."

"You have no idea?"

"No."

"Have you ever seen them before?"

"No."

"Would you like to go to the hospital and get that shoulder looked at?"

"N—I think that would be a fine idea."

They took him to a hospital on Second Avenue, where Tally walked him down to an area where a lot of people were being treated for wounds.

"What happened here?" Tally asked a doctor.

"Big fight on Broadway," the man answered. "We're swamped here. What have you got?"

"Bullet wound."

"Bad?" the doctor asked, looking at Decker.

"Not too bad," Decker said.

"I can have a nurse dress it," the doctor said to Lieutenant Tally.

"That'll be fine." Tally turned to Decker and said, "I'll wait for you outside and take you back to your hotel."

"I appreciate it."

"Come with me," the doctor said.

He led Decker to a small cubicle with a table and chair and said, "Sit on the table and wait. A nurse will be right with you."

Decker nodded. He waited a full ten minutes, and then a woman entered and pulled a white curtain closed so that they wouldn't be disturbed. Decker was going to say something, but when she turned, the words caught in his throat.

"Hello," she said.

She was beautiful, sultry, even in white. She had brown eyes, with heavy eyebrows, and a lush mouth. She was about twenty-four, five five and slender. At the moment her beautiful face looked a little sad, as if she'd seen a lot of pain that night—or that year.

"What's wrong?" she asked.

"I . . . got shot."

"I know that, silly," she said. "I mean, why were you staring?"

"Was I?" he asked. "I'm sorry."

She almost said something, then just gave her head a little shake and moved toward him.

"Let me have a look at that."

She leaned over him to look at the wound, and he could smell her, her hair. She must have been on duty for a while, because he could smell her sweat, a scent that was not at all unpleasant.

She slid his jacket down and looked at his shoulder.

"This doesn't look too bad."

"That's what I told the doctor."

"Let's get your shirt off," she said. "Help me."

"Sure."

Together they got his shirt off. When she saw the scars on his body, she gasped.

"Well," she said, "you've been through this before."

"Once or twice."

"I can count," she said. She looked the wound over and said, "The bullet is still in there. You didn't tell the doctor that. I'll have to get him."

She started away, and he grabbed her arm.

"You do it."

"You trust me?"

He moved his hand from her arm to her hand and said, "I trust these hands."

She smiled at him and said, "OK, cowboy. Let's get it done."

After she got the bullet out, she cleaned and dressed the wound, then stepped back to admire her handiwork.

"Not bad, even if I do say so myself." She was smiling, but there was a touch of sadness in her eyes.

"What's your name?" he asked her.

"Linda Hamilton."

"I'm Decker," he said, putting his hand out.

She hesitated a moment, then put her hand in his.

"Thank you," he said, shaking it.

"You're very welcome."

She helped him get his shirt and jacket back on. Then she smiled at him again. "Good luck," she said.

"You didn't even ask me how this happened."

"I'd be lying if I said I wasn't curious," she said,

"but I'm afraid I don't have the time. I still have an hour to go on my shift, and we are very busy."

She had a strand of hair caught on her left eyebrow so that every time she blinked, it moved. He reached up with his left hand and freed it.

"Goodbye," she said.

"Goodbye."

She drew the white curtain open and stepped out. He watched her walk down the hall.

Outside, Lieutenant Tally was waiting, smoking a cigarette.

"Finished already?"

"Yes."

"Let's take a ride to my office and talk a little bit. Feel up to it?"

"Sure. Let's go."

Police headquarters was otherwise known as the Central Office. It was located on Mulberry Street, between Houston and Bleecker streets. It was a handsome structure of white marble that extended through the block to Mott Street, where its front was brick.

The Central Office housed the offices of the commissioners and their clerks, the superintendent, the street-cleaning bureau, the detective squad, the chief surgeon and the rogues' gallery. The building was also connected to each of the city's thirty-five station houses by special telegraph wire.

Tally was assigned to the detective squad. He didn't have an office but a desk in an office full of desks.

"Cigarette?" he asked, sitting behind his desk.

"Thanks," Decker said, accepting one and lighting it from Tally's.

"You got anything else to tell me, Mr. Decker?"

"Just Decker, no *mister.*"

"All right, Decker. What else is there?"

"That's all, Lieutenant. I didn't know those two, and I don't know why they would try to kill me."

"Well, take my advice," Tally said. "The only reason those two would try to kill you is because they were hired to. That means that the man behind them might still want you."

"I suppose so."

"Might be time for you to leave town."

"I just got here."

"And already you've had more fun than most people do in a lifetime," Tally said. "You want a ride back to the hotel?"

"No, I think I'd like a ride back to the hospital."

"Feeling all right?"

"Fine. I met someone inside who's very curious about how I got shot."

"That makes two of us," Tally said. "Oh, here. This is yours."

He handed Decker Dover's knife.

"I cleaned it."

"Thanks," Decker said. "What about my guns?"

"They'll be returned to your hotel in the morning, but your rifle is still in your room."

Decker put the knife into his coat pocket and thanked Tally again.

"Here's my card," Tally said. "If you think of something or have any more trouble, let me know."

"Sure."

"Oh, one more thing, Decker."

"What's that?"

"Don't think I'm buying this act of yours," the lieutenant said. "I'm just giving you some time to think it over before we talk again—and we will be talking again."

"I'll look forward to it, Lieutenant."

Chapter Five

While he was waiting for Linda Hamilton to come out, Decker thought back again to that time he and Dover "volunteered" to be deputies for a sheriff in a small Arizona town . . .

"Either one of you ever been to these parts before?" the sheriff asked.

They'd been out about three hours. The sheriff had picked up the trail just outside of town, and they'd been following it this far.

"Never been," Dover answered.

The sheriff looked at Decker then and asked, "Your friend do all the talking for both of you?"

"Only when it comes to volunteering."

"You're both kind of young, aren't you?"

"For what?" Dover asked.

The sheriff, a gray-haired man in his fifties, hesitated a moment, then said, "For a lot of things, I guess . . ."

After five hours they caught up to the robbers. Thinking they were in the clear, the men had stopped to care for one of their number who'd been shot.

When the firing started, the sheriff, Dover and Decker jumped from their horses and took cover. There were some spirited exchanges. Then the sheriff said, "Cover me." They tried, but he only took five steps before he was hit by a barrage of bullets.

"Hey, deputies!" a man's voice shouted. "Your boss is dead. Are those badges important enough for you to die for?"

Dover and Decker exchanged glances.

"It ain't the badges, Deck," Dover said. "It's what they represent."

"And what's that?"

"Justice."

"When did you become such a stickler for justice?"

Dover gave Decker a real serious look and said, "When I put on this badge."

Decker stared at Dover. Then he shook his head slowly and said, "All right, let's get 'em."

Then the two young men figured out their approach. In an hour they killed three of the gang and secured the remaining two for the trip back to town. After they tied the body of the sheriff to his horse, they returned to town with him, the two gang members and the bank's money . . .

Dover had stayed on as the new sheriff, but Decker turned down his offer of a deputy's badge and moved on.

Decker drifted for a while, was almost hanged for a crime he didn't commit and became a bounty hunter.

When he met him almost five years later, Dover was also a bounty hunter. He had soured on a lawman's high risk for low pay and lower esteem. The shine of the badge had dulled for Dover, but bounty hunting still satisfied his desire for justice . . . and his new-found desire for money . . .

* * *

"Hello."

The voice disturbed his reverie.

He looked at Linda Hamilton, still wearing white but without her white cap. Her brown hair was attractively arranged. Her eyes, now a little tired, were still sad.

"Hello," he said. "I thought you might be hungry."

"I usually have something to eat after my shift."

"I'm a little hungry myself."

"I usually eat alone," she said. After a moment she added, "But I *could* use a little company tonight."

He smiled and said, "Good, and as a token of my appreciation, I'll buy."

Chapter Six

"Am I entitled to have my curiosity satisfied?" she asked over dinner.

She had suggested a small all-night restaurant a few blocks from the hospital. Decker felt naked during the walk, since he was armed only with Dover's newly honed lucky piece. Still, she apparently made the walk herself several evenings a week. Under the circumstances he felt he could afford to take the walk once. Besides, she was there to protect him.

When they entered the restaurant, which was hardly more than a hole in the wall, the waitress greeted her warmly and by name. She was about Linda's age, but the similarity ended there. The waitress wasn't anywhere near as attractive as Linda Hamilton.

"Well?"

"Well what?" he asked.

"My curiosity?"

"You mean, now that you're off duty?"

She smiled and said, "Yes, now that I'm off duty."

"Ask."

"First, who shot you?"

"Big ugly fella named Clyde."

She frowned and said, "Why?"

"He didn't say."

"Did you ask him?"

"I did."

"And what did he say?"

"He said the time for having fun was over."

"You don't know very much about why you were shot, do you?"

"No."

"That must be very frustrating."

"It is."

"What about the other times?"

"What other times?"

"The other times you were shot?"

"Oh, those other times. I generally knew why it was happening."

"Why?"

"Because somebody was trying to kill me."

"I saw two bullet-wound scars and a knife scar on your torso."

"Oh, you didn't see my back," he said. "There's another bullet and a knife scar there, and if you want to talk about my legs—"

"I don't think I do," she said.

"Sorry."

The waitress came with the eggs and bacon they had ordered because of the late—and early—hour.

"Is life that violent out west for everyone?"

"Only if you go looking for it."

"And you do?"

"I couldn't be in my business if I didn't."

"And what business is that?"

He hesitated a moment, wondering why he'd led the conversation around to this. Then he told her.

"I'm a bounty hunter."

"Really?" she asked. "That sounds very interesting."

It took him a moment to figure out that she didn't

believe him. He wasn't all that sure he wanted to convince her.

"Sometimes," he said.

"Like tonight?"

He decided it was time to grimace a little.

"Your shoulder hurt?" she asked. Her concern was so genuine he felt guilty about faking the grimace. "Maybe we should have had the doctor look at it."

"No, no, it's fine really," he said. "Tell me about you. How old are you?"

"Twenty-five," she said. "Why did you ask that?"

"I wanted to see if you'd answer honestly."

"What makes you think I did?"

"I figured you for twenty-four."

"I'm flattered."

They finished eating and left the restaurant. Decker paid.

In front he said, "Can I see you home?"

"I appreciate the meal, Mr. Decker, and the company—and having my curiosity satisfied, sort of—but I don't think we know each other that well yet."

He was pleased that she had used *yet*.

"Well, if my shoulder starts to act up, where can I find you?"

She smiled and said, "At the hospital."

"Be careful going home, then."

"That sounds like better advice for you than me," she said.

"I intend to follow it."

"Good night, Mr. Decker."

"Not Mr. Decker," he said. "Just Decker."

She started to walk away. Then she turned and said, "Tell me something, Just Decker."

"What?"

"Are you really a bounty hunter?"

"Yep."

She regarded him for a moment. Then she said, "Interesting," and walked off down the street.

As he watched her walk away, Decker said, "Interesting," too. Then he started back to his hotel.

Chapter Seven

An insistent knocking woke Decker the next morning. He staggered to it, wondering if Linda Hamilton had decided that they *did* know each other that well, after all. Then he remembered that he hadn't told her the name of his hotel.

It was Lieutenant Tally, bearing gifts.

"Your guns," he said, holding them out.

"Thanks." Decker reached for them with one hand.

"Not so fast," Tally said, holding back.

"More conversation?"

"If you don't mind."

Decker waved him in and moved back to the bed to sit down.

Tally entered and closed the doors. He put the guns on the nearby dresser.

"Is this going to take long?" Decker asked.

"That depends."

"How about doing it over breakfast?"

Tally shrugged.

"I don't mind. Who's paying?"

"I guess I am."

"I'll wait downstairs while you get dressed," Tally said. "Don't disappoint me."

"I'll be along as soon as I can. I can't move around real fast with this wound, you know."

"The way you look, you've been through this enough times to know all the shortcuts."

Tally left, and Decker washed up and got dressed. He wanted to put the shoulder rig on, but one of the straps put pressure on his wound. He took the New Line out of the holster and dropped it into the pocket of one of his new coats.

Tally was waiting in the hotel lobby.

"Hotel dining room?" he asked.

"I was warned against it. Let's go to a small restaurant I found last night. It'll be a long walk, but I need to stretch my legs, anyway."

As they left the hotel, Decker saw Billy Rosewood standing out front. As Rosewood spotted Tally, he immediately hid his face.

He needn't have bothered. Tally saw him.

"Hello, Billy."

"Good morning, Lieutenant. Mr. Decker."

"You two know each other?" Tally asked.

"Billy gave me a ride from the train station."

Tally gave Rosewood a meaningful look.

"Selling guns again, Billy?" he asked. "I warned you about that—"

"Hey, hey," Decker said, "the gun's mine. The kid had nothing to do with it."

"Sure," Tally said, "you cowboys always carry ladies' specials."

Tally turned back to Billy Rosewood.

"What are you doing around here? No business today?"

Rosewood looked past Tally at Decker.

"He's waiting for me," Decker said. "I needed somebody to show me around town."

"Well, you picked the right boy. Billy knows all the spots in town, don't you, Billy?"

"What spots?" Decker asked.

"The trouble spots."

"Oh, I don't want to see those. Billy said he was going to show me the best churches."

"Churches," Tally said, nodding his head.

"Wait here, Billy," Decker said. "The lieutenant and I are going to have some breakfast."

"Sure, Mr. Decker."

Tally gave Rosewood a pointed look and then followed Decker.

"Who showed you this place?" Tally asked. He looked around with disapproval. Decker noticed for the first time that Tally's suit was a lot more expensive than his—a *lot* more.

"A lady friend."

"You've been in town one day," Tally said, "and so far you've found Billy Rosewood, a lady friend, a hole-in-the-wall restaurant and a mess of trouble. You work fast, Decker."

"Listen, Lieutenant, I haven't even started to work yet."

"Aha. Then you are here working."

"Let's get a table."

Tally looked around and saw that the place was empty.

"That shouldn't be too difficult."

There were two waitresses working. One of them was the same one who had served Decker and Linda Hamilton the night before. She came over and smiled at him.

"Hello. You're Linda's friend."

"That's right."

"The eggs must have been good last night."

"Are they still good?"

"The best."

"We'll have some."

"This way."

Tally gave his chair a good close scrutiny before sitting in it.

"I assume you're used to better places than this," Decker said.

"I usually frequent, uh, cleaner establishments, yes."

"Wait until you taste the eggs," Decker said. "You might find cleaner, but you won't find better."

"Coffee?" the waitress asked.

"Yes," Decker said, "two cups."

"One clean one."

The waitress gave Tally a hurt look and went to fill the order.

"You're a mean man," Decker said. "You hurt her feelings."

"She'll live."

"You have some questions for me?"

"Did you remember anything else from last night?"

"Not a thing."

"Boil had six hundred dollars on him."

"What about his brother?"

"Boil carried all the money for both of them."

"Oh," Decker said, "for a minute there I was almost flattered."

"Anyway," Tally said, "it looks like the brothers were paid to kill you."

"That's nice," Decker said.

The waitress brought the coffee and the eggs. She slammed a cup down in front of Tally and said, "Here's the clean one!"

After she left, Tally said, "Who wants to kill you that bad?"

"I just got to town, Lieutenant," Decker said. "I don't know anybody."

"Well, somebody knows you. Somebody had them at the station waiting for you."

Decker decided it was time for him to give the lieutenant something to occupy his time.

"Wait a minute."

"You remember something?" Tally asked. He was eating the eggs without a hint of complaint.

"Yeah. The big one, Boil . . . he called me Dover."

"Well, I guess they thought you were this Dover guy."

"I guess so. Maybe you can find out if a man named Dover came into town on the same train I did."

"I'll check on it after breakfast."

"How are the eggs?"

Tally stopped short as he was shoveling the last of his eggs into his mouth and said, "Uh, they're not bad."

"Here," Decker said, dropping some money on the table, "eat mine."

"Where are you going?"

"I told you," Decker said, standing up, "I'm going to church."

Chapter Eight

Decker found Billy Rosewood still waiting in front of the hotel.

"Are you in trouble with the police, Mr. Decker?" he asked.

"I picked up a bullet last night without paying for it."

"A bullet? From where?"

"From that little gun you got me."

"Well, don't blame me," Rosewood said. "I didn't think you were going to shoot *yourself* with it."

"I didn't—It's a long story, Billy. Wait for me here. I've got to check at the desk."

Decker went inside and approached the desk.

"Are there any telegraph messages for me?"

"Mr. Decker? Yes, sir." The man turned, took an envelope out of his box and slid it across the desk to Decker.

"Thank you."

"Uh, Mr. Decker," the man said, "we have another room available if you like—"

"*No.* The one I have is fine."

"But the incident—"

"The incident was my fault. I should watch who I let into my room."

"That's very kind of you, sir."

"Forget it."

Decker went out to Rosewood's cab and said,

"Let's go for a ride. I don't know where yet. I'll let you know."

"You're the boss."

Decker got into the cab, and Rosewood climbed up top and got started. Decker opened the envelope and read Duke's telegram.

DECKER,

PAPER ON READY RECENT. KILLED THREE PEOPLE UNDER THREE DIFFERENT NAMES. READY IS REAL NAME. DON'T KNOW MUCH ABOUT HIM, PERSONALLY.

SAY HELLO TO BOOKMAN FOR ME. 483 BROOME STREET. ENJOY NEW YORK.

DUKE

Decker stuck his head out of the window and shouted up to Rosewood. "You know where Broome Street is?"

"Course!"

"Four-eight-three," Decker called out.

"Right," Rosewood said, waving a hand.

Chapter Nine

In a rooming house on Delancey Street, Oakley Ready sat naked on a bed counting his money. He still had about sixty-five hundred dollars left from the last bank he had robbed—just before Dover got onto his trail. He was out travel money and the money he'd been spreading behind him, trying to make sure Dover ended up dead.

He knew that the men he'd paid in Harrison City had failed to kill Dover because he'd read about the shooting in the St. Martin's Hotel in the newspapers. The two men he'd hired to watch the train station were dead, too. Ready hadn't known either town, or he'd have been able to hire better men.

He knew somebody in New York, though. He would get in touch with him today. It had taken him three days to find out where the guy was. Through this man he'd get some quality guns to go after Dover.

Once he had Dover taken care of, he'd be able to trade in this Delancey Street rooming house for a respectable hotel. He hadn't seen much of New York since arriving, but he'd seen enough to know that it was his kind of town. There was plenty of money to be had, and plenty of places to spend it.

The girl on the other side of the bed rolled over and looked at Ready, then at the money. Her brown hair was tousled, and her lips slightly swollen.

"How much have you got left?" she asked.

"Enough," he said, smiling at her.

He'd picked her up waiting tables in a restaurant. She wasn't a beauty, but she was attractive and had a nice, solid body. He liked women with solid bodies.

The sheet fell away from her as she sat up, and he stared at her breasts. Then she reached for the money, and he grabbed her wrist and held it so tightly that bones started to grind together.

"Jesus—" she said, wincing in pain.

"We'll get along fine, Marcy, as long as you re-member one thing."

"W-what?"

He let go of her wrist and said, "Don't touch my money."

"A-all r-right," she said, rubbing her wrist.

He swept the money off the bed onto the floor, then got onto the bed with her.

"Here," he said, taking her hand, "let me kiss it and make it better."

Only it wasn't her wrist that he started kissing.

Chapter Ten

The door of the second-floor offices said, WALTER BOOKMAN, nothing else. All the other doors had names and occupations on them, but not Bookman's.

Decker knocked. He heard a chair squeak and footsteps approaching. Then the door opened.

The man in the doorway was big, over six feet, with a bushy black beard and an ill-fitting suit. Decker thought he'd probably have a lot of trouble finding a suit that would close Over his belly. He was chewing, as if Decker had interrupted his breakfast. There was some grease on his beard. He was a rough-looking man until you looked at his eyes. They were blue, and gentle looking. They were probably a disadvantage in his business.

"Yeah, what?" His voice fit his eyes rather than his appearance. Another disadvantage.

"Mr. Bookman?"

"That's right."

"I bring greetings from a friend."

"Oh, yeah? Who?"

"Duke Ballard."

"Duke," Bookman said, nodding his head. He chewed the last of the food in his mouth and asked, "Who are you?"

"Decker."

"Oh, yeah," Bookman said, looking him up and down. "So you're Decker. I heard of you."

"I never heard of you."

"That's the first good news I've had all week," Bookman said. "Come on in and shut the door behind you."

Bookman backed away, and Decker entered, closing the door as instructed.

Bookman went around behind his desk and sat down. On the desk in front of him were a plate of bacon and eggs and another with biscuits and butter. There was also a pot of coffee. The room smelled as if he'd cooked it all himself.

"Want some?" Bookman asked.

"No, thanks."

"I got a stove in the other room. It's no trouble."

"That's OK," Decker said. "I had breakfast."

"Coffee?"

"Sure."

Bookman took a cup out of a bottom drawer and handed it to Decker. Decker blew some dust out of it before pouring himself a cup of coffee. Then he sat in a straight-backed chair in front of Bookman's desk.

"What can I do for you, then?" Bookman asked. "You still a man hunter?"

"Yes."

"Is that why you're here?"

"Yes."

"Who are you looking for—oh, you don't mind if I finish eating while we talk, do you?"

"No, go right ahead," Decker said. He took the poster out of his pocket and unfolded it. "This is the man I'm looking for, Bookman."

Bookman wiped his hand on his coat and took the poster. He dropped it on the table next to his plate.

"You know him?" Decker asked.

"I've heard of him, yeah." Bookman picked up a biscuit and buttered it.

"I think he's in New York."

"What makes you think that?"

"Turn that over."

Bookman turned the poster over and read the list of cities.

"In Harrison City, Ready had three men kill a friend of mine named Dover."

"Another man hunter?"

"Right."

"They gun him?"

"In the back."

Bookman made a face.

"Then you're not after the bounty."

"Don't make me sound so noble," Decker said. "If I get him, I'll take the money."

Bookman's smile was fleeting. Then he said, "OK."

"I don't know this town, Bookman. I need help."

"Where are you staying?"

"A hotel on Twenty-third Street—uh, the St. Martin's."

Bookman was nodding to himself, chewing on a piece of biscuit.

"All right, Decker. I'll see what I can find out." Decker stood up and said, "Thanks."

"Don't forget your paper."

Decker reached over and picked it up.

"You don't mind if I check you out with Duke, do you, Decker?"

"Be my guest."

Decker started for the door and was stopped by Bookman's voice.

"Hey, Decker."

"Yeah?"

"Did he try for you yet?"

"Yeah, at my hotel. Two of them."

"They both dead?"

"Yep."

"They know who you were?"

"They thought I was Dover."

"Who'd you talk to from the police?"

"Lieutenant Tally."

"Tally," Bookman repeated, but Decker couldn't read anything in his tone.

"You know him?"

"I'll get in touch with you at your hotel."

Decker hesitated a moment, then nodded and went outside, where Rosewood waited by his cab.

"Where to?" he asked when Decker appeared.

"I don't know . . . wait, yes I do."

"Where?"

"Show me some churches."

"Churches?" Rosewood asked. "What kind of churches?"

Decker grinned and said, "The kind that serve liquor, of course."

Chapter Eleven

Rosewood stopped his cab and stepped down, and Decker stepped out.

"Where are we?"

"Printing House Square—This is where all of New York's newspapers are located," Rosewood explained. "We're at the east side of City Hall Park and the north end of Park Row. See that statue over there?"

"I see it."

"Ol' Ben Franklin." Rosewood turned to Decker and said with a conspiratorial smile, "This is also where all the best saloons are. Come on."

They began walking, stopping into a saloon for a drink, then moving on to the next. Rosewood explained to Decker about the newspaper industry in New York.

There were approximately twelve morning newspapers, seven evening papers, ten semiweekly tabloids, two hundred weeklies and about twenty-five magazines.

"That's the *Herald*," Rosewood said, pointing to a magnificent white marble structure. It was easily the most conspicuous building in the square. It was owned by James Gordon Bennett and located on the corner of Broadway and Ann Streets.

Later they passed the *Tribune*, which had been founded by Horace Greeley. It was situated on the corners of Nassau and Spruce Streets.

When they were in a saloon, sitting at a table with a cold beer before them, Rosewood said, "Listen to the conversations."

And so Decker listened for several minutes, eavesdropping on three of four different conversations. Each centered on the same thing.

"Money," Billy Rosewood said. "That's why every once in a while I come down here, park and saloon-hop. I can smell the money in the air."

Decker had wondered why Rosewood, dressed as plainly as he was, had not drawn any curious glances whenever they entered one of the Printing House Square saloons. Now he knew.

"They're used to you, aren't they?" he asked.

"Yeah, I've been doing this for a while," Rosewood said. "They objected at first. I even got thrown out of one or two places, but they finally came to accept me, like I was one of the tables or chairs."

"And me?"

Rosewood shrugged.

"I guess they accept you because you're with me."

"You ever take anyone else hopping with you?"

"No."

"Why me?"

Rosewood shrugged again.

"Guess I never liked anyone well enough."

"I'm flattered."

"Would you like to tell me about last night?"

Decker thought a moment, then decided to go ahead and tell him about Boil and his brother. In fact, he told him everything he'd told Tally. He did not, however, tell Rosewood that he had told Bookman.

"And you don't know why they wanted to kill you?"

"I have to assume that they just mistook me for someone else."

"So what *are* you doing in New York?"

Decker shrugged.

"I've never been here before. I thought it was time."

"Uh-huh, you're just on vacation."

"That's right."

"And I suppose you're a peace-loving, churchgoing man who just got lucky last night against two killers."

"I never said that."

"Well, at least you don't think I'm stupid."

"I never said or thought that either." Decker checked the time. "Any of these places serve decent food?"

"Yeah, as a matter of fact, this one serves real good steak and onion sandwiches, which go great with cold beer."

"All right," Decker said, "I'll buy you lunch."

"I thought you might," Rosewood said, smiling, "so when I went to the bar for the beers, I ordered for both of us."

Chapter Twelve

Ready left the girl, Marcy, in his room with the money. He knew she wouldn't dare take any. Hell, she wouldn't even touch it. But she'd stay around as long as there was the slightest chance she might end up getting some of it.

Ready caught a horsecar to Fourteenth Street, then walked up to Tenth Avenue. He found the building he was looking for and entered a shop in it. From what he could see, all that was sold there was junk.

"Can I help you?" asked a man behind the counter. He was in his fifties, with gray hair and a barrel chest. He looked at Ready from over a pair of wire-framed glasses.

"Yeah," Ready said, "maybe you can. I'm looking for Albert Bolan."

"Yeah?"

"Do you know him?"

"Maybe. What are you looking for him for?"

"Friend of mine is a friend of his," Ready said. "He told me to look him up."

"What for?" the man asked. "Business or pleasure?"

"Business."

"What kind of business?"

Ready took out a hundred-dollar bill and said, "The kind that pays."

"You're not the law, are you?"

"Do you know any lawmen who carry around this kind of money, friend?"

The man thought for a moment, then came to a decision.

"Flip that sign on the door around so it says, CLOSED," he instructed.

Ready walked to the door and turned the sign around. Then he asked, "Are you Bolan?"

"I'm Bolan. Come on in the back room. And bring your friend with the zeros with you."

A little later on, Oakley Ready left the junk shop, turning the sign around so that it read, OPEN, again. He walked down Fourteenth Street to a point where he could catch a horsecar again.

He was a couple of hundred dollars lighter than he was when he went in, but by this time tomorrow he should have two professional guns good enough to take care of Dover.

If he didn't, his new friend Albert Bolan was going to owe him a refund—and an explanation.

Chapter Thirteen

Rosewood dropped Decker off in front of his hotel.

"Thanks for the tour, Billy."

"Will you want me later tonight?"

"I don't think—wait a minute."

"What?"

"I'll tell you what," Decker said after a moment. "Will you be available at two a.m.?"

"Sure, if you want."

"You know that hospital I told you I was at?"

"Sure, on Second Avenue."

"Go there at two and pick up a nurse."

"Sure," Billy said, grinning, "just any nurse?"

"Quiet, and listen. I'll describe her." Decker described Linda Hamilton as well as he could, and Rosewood laughed.

"What's so funny?"

"The only time I ever heard a man describe a woman that well, he was in love with her."

"Don't be a dope. I only met her yesterday."

"I know," Rosewood said, still grinning.

"Stop grinning like a fool. After you've picked her up, take her to—what's a decent restaurant that's open that time of night?"

"I know one," Rosewood said and gave Decker instructions how to get there.

"Good. Bring her there."

"Want me to have someone pick you up and take you there?" Rosewood asked.

"Like who?"

"A friend."

"An expensive friend?"

"You don't pay him, you pay me—after."

"I appreciate that, Billy."

"I feel it's my responsibility to see that you enjoy my city, Mr. Decker."

"No *mister*, Billy . . . just Decker."

"All right, Decker. I'll see you tonight."

Decker waved and went into the hotel lobby. As he entered, he saw the clerk behind the desk nod to someone. There was a man sitting in the lobby, and he rose and approached Decker, who put his hand over the .32 in his pocket.

"Decker?" the man said.

"That's right."

"I'm from Bookman."

"Yeah?"

"He sent me with a message."

The man was tall and thin, well dressed and impeccably groomed. He didn't appear to be armed, but that might have been due to the work of a good tailor.

"All right," Decker said, "let's go to my room."

They went up to the second floor, to the door of Decker's room.

"After you," Decker said, and the man entered ahead of him.

Decker came in behind him and took the .32 from his pocket. He pressed the barrel against the man's back and closed the door behind them.

"What's this?" the man asked.

"I'm just being careful," Decker said. "Put your hands up."

The man obeyed, and Decker searched him. He found a .38-caliber Colt under his arm, and nothing else. He returned the .32 to his pocket and held the man's .38.

"OK, sit on the bed."

The man did so.

"What's your message?"

"Bookman thought you might need some help."

"Why is that?"

He did some checking on the man you're looking for."

"And what he found out made him think I needed a bodyguard?"

"I guess so."

"Well, you go back and tell him to do just what we agreed that he'd do. I don't need a baby sitter."

The man stood up and straightened his coat.

"My gun, please?"

"What's your name?"

"Largo," the man said, "Jim Largo."

"All right, Mr. Largo," Decker said and handed him his gun back. "Tell Bookman I appreciate the offer."

"I'll tell him."

"I assume he hasn't found my man yet."

"No," Largo said, "he hasn't found him."

"What would Ready have done when he got here?" Decker asked out loud.

"I don't know."

"He would have done the same thing I did," Decker said, talking more to himself, although loud enough for the other man to hear.

"Gone to see Bookman?" Largo said, shaking his head. "Nobody but you has seen—"

"No, not Bookman," Decker said, "but somebody like him." Decker looked at Largo and said, "There are . . . others in New York who supply the same services that Bookman supplies, aren't there?"

"I suppose so."

"Ask Bookman to check on them, see if they've had any requests for help from out-of-towners."

"All right," Largo said. He started for the door, opened it and then turned to look at Decker. "I don't like having my gun taken away from me."

Decker returned the man's stare and said, "Next time you come to see me, don't wear it."

Chapter Fourteen

At 1:45 a.m., Decker found a horse-drawn cab waiting in front of his hotel, with a young man leaning against it. As he approached it, the young man straightened.

"You Decker?"

"I'm Decker. What's your name?"

"Archie."

"OK, Archie, let's go."

Decker climbed inside, and Archie up top. In the dark, Decker wasn't quite sure what route the cab was taking, and he kept his hand in his pocket, over the .32. He was suspicious of everyone these days.

Finally, Decker saw a street sign for Forty-third Street and recalled that Rosewood had said this was the street the restaurant was on. Moments later they pulled up in front.

He stepped out of the cab and saw that this was a far cry from the little restaurant where he and Linda Hamilton had first shared a meal.

"This place is gonna cost you plenty," Archie said with a smirk. "I hope the girl is worth it."

"She is."

Archie looked up and down the deserted street and said, "I hope she shows up."

"So do I," Decker said. "I'll be inside, Archie."

"OK, boss."

Decker entered the restaurant and was met at the door by a man in a tuxedo.

"Sir?"

"Decker."

"Yes, sir. This way, please."

Decker followed the man to a table, where the man held his chair for him.

"Your waiter will be here shortly."

"No hurry," Decker said, "I'm waiting for a young lady."

"Ah," the man said with no expression and left Decker to his own devices.

Decker admired the interior, which was all crystal and leather. As deserted as it was outside, inside it was very busy. There were no other empty tables as far as he could see.

He checked a clock on the wall. It was ten minutes past two. He was worrying that Billy Rosewood had not been persuasive enough when she suddenly came into view, following the same man in the tuxedo. She was wearing her uniform, and a stern look.

"Your companion, sir," the man said, holding her chair for her.

"Thank you," she said.

"I will send your waiter over."

Decker nodded, and the man left them.

"I will never forgive you for this," Linda said.

"For what exactly?" he asked. "I hope Billy wasn't too—"

"Not for Billy," she said. "For this . . . this place."

"What's wrong with it?"

"Nothing. It's one of the most expensive restaurants in New York, which is why they stay open so late, in order to accommodate all of their patrons."

"Then why so unforgiving?"

"Because you let me come to this beautiful place dressed like . . . like this."

He smiled at her and put his hand over hers.

"Believe me, Linda," Decker said, "you are the most beautiful thing in this beautiful place."

"You're impossible."

"No," he said, "I'm not."

"What happened?" Bookman asked.

"He took my gun."

Bookman frowned and looked up from his late snack of a whole chicken and vegetables.

"I wouldn't have thought you'd admit that so easily," he said, pointing at Largo with a chicken leg.

"What?"

"That a man took your gun away from you."

"Why not?" Largo said, grinning coldly. "It means he's good."

"The word I get from Duke Ballard is that he's the best," Bookman said.

Largo smiled.

"Best in the West."

"Meaning what?" Bookman asked. "That you're the best in the East?"

Largo shrugged.

"Anyway, his idea is sound," Bookman said. "Check on Sadler, Liston . . . and Bolan."

"It'll be Bolan," Largo said.

"Yeah," Bookman said, "you're probably right, but check them all, anyway."

"All right."

"And Largo?"

Largo stopped on his way to the door.

"Yes?"

"Try and control your competitive streak where Decker is concerned. He's a friend of a friend."

"A friend of a friend of yours," Largo said, "not mine."

Later Decker and Linda went to his room.

"I don't feel right about this," she said, standing with her back up against the door.

"To tell you the truth," he said, "neither do I."

"Really?"

He smiled and said, "Really, I'm not what you'd call a lady's man."

"You could have fooled me."

"No," he said, shaking his head, "if I've seemed that way at all, it's because of you."

"Of me?"

"I've never . . . been so affected by a woman on such short acquaintance."

"You mean the other night?"

He nodded.

"But that wasn't even—we didn't even get acquainted."

"That's all right," he said. "It happened as soon as I saw you. You're very beautiful, Linda, and you had such a . . . gentle touch."

"I . . . was doing my job."

She was still standing against the door, and he could see the tension in her shoulders. He picked up her coat, walked up to her and put his hand on the doorknob.

"I'll have Billy take you home."

"Home? You mean you don't want—"

"Whatever I want," he said, "I want you to want

it, too. I think we both feel a little too awkward tonight."

She frowned at him and said, "You're a strange man, Decker."

"Maybe you won't think so," he said, handing her her coat, "after we become better acquainted."

Studying his face, she said, "Maybe I won't."

She stepped away from the door so that he could open it, and then he stepped away to allow her to precede him.

"Maybe we could dine again soon," he said.

"Maybe," she said.

He walked her down to the lobby and to the front door. Billy Rosewood was waiting outside.

"Good night," he said.

"Thank you for dinner."

He smiled and said, "Next time I'll give you time to dress properly."

She smiled back and started through the door. As the door closed, she turned and looked at him through the glass.

He pushed the door open a crack, and she said, "Tomorrow is my day off. Would you like to go to a baseball game?"

Chapter Fifteen

When Decker came out of his hotel the following morning, Billy Rosewood was waiting out front.

"Didn't do so good last night, did you?" Rosewood asked.

"And what makes you say that?"

"Well, the lady went home kind of early, didn't she?"

"That's because we have a date today," Decker said.

"Oh? To do what?"

"To see a baseball game."

"How romantic. That won't be until noon. You want breakfast?"

"Sure."

"Come on," Rosewood said. "I know a place."

The East River Bridge was to be constructed in five parts. The central span of the bridge would be 1,595 feet long when it was completed. There would also be a span on each side—the Manhattan side and the Brooklyn side—from the tower to the anchorage, 940 feet in length. Then there would be approaches on each side.

Rosewood took Decker to a restaurant on Roosevelt Street. They got a seat by the window, from where they could see the tower.

"What is that?" Decker asked.

"Right now it's a tower," Rosewood said, "but when it's done, it will be a bridge, a suspension bridge connecting Manhattan to Brooklyn."

"I thought this was New York."

"They're both New York," Rosewood said, "but this side is called Manhattan Island, while the other side is called Brooklyn. That bridge will span the East River and connect the two."

"Amazing," Decker said.

When the waiter came, they ordered lunch, and Rosewood explained what little he knew about baseball.

"I'm not a fan or anything," Rosewood said, "and I've never been to a game, but as I understand it, the object of the game is to hit a ball that is thrown by a man, uh, with a stick that they call a bat."

"And what do you do after you hit it?"

"Uh . . . run."

"To where?"

Rosewood frowned and said, "You'd better wait until you and the lady go to the game, Decker. She'll be able to explain it to you better."

"I'm sure she will," Decker said. "She couldn't do it any worse."

Rosewood knew the way to Linda Hamilton's residence because he'd taken her home the night before.

"It's in Five Points, on Mulberry Street," Rosewood said. "Bad part of town."

"What's she doing there?"

"Probably she can't afford to live any place else."

"She has a good job."

Rosewood shrugged and said, "She must have been born there."

When Rosewood stopped in front of Linda's building, Decker got out.

"Second floor rear," Rosewood called down.

"Got it."

Decker entered the building and climbed the rickety steps to the second floor. Apparently there were two apartments on each floor. He walked to the rear and knocked.

"Hello," Linda said as she opened the door.

"Hi," he said.

They stood there a few seconds and then he said, "Can I come in?"

"Oh, I'm sorry," she said, stepping back. "Of course, come in."

He entered, and she closed the door. The place was modestly furnished, but it was very clean and well kept.

"Not much, I know."

"I've seen worse."

"Have you?" she asked. "Where?"

"All over the West," he said. "In fact, in some places this would be thought of as luxurious."

"I haven't been anywhere but here," she said. "I'd love to travel." She looked at Decker and said, "When you're born in Five Points, all you can do is hope to get out one day."

"You have a good job," he said, echoing what he'd said to Rosewood. "Surely you can save some money."

"I am trying," she said. "Shall we go? The game starts at noon."

"I'm afraid you'll have to explain this game to me," he said as they walked to the door. "In detail."

"Oh, I will," she said. "I just love watching them play. I'm sure you'll like it too."

"I'm sure I will," Decker said, without conviction.

Chapter Sixteen

As it turned out, he did enjoy it.

He found himself wondering how the man with the bat could possibly hit the ball, given the speed with which it was being thrown. Also, he wondered why there were times a man could hit the ball so solidly, and yet get nothing for it, and other times he didn't hit the ball at all and was awarded "first base."

"I can't quite understand the rules of this game. It must take years of practice to play it correctly," he said to her at one point.

"I'm sure it does," she said.

New York was playing St. Louis. She explained that they were in something called "the National League," the first really organized "league." The game had been played by amateurs until as recently as 1869 and then had became a professional sport.

"You mean they get paid to play a game?"

"Oh, yes, indeed."

"How do you know so much about baseball?"

"I used to see one of the players," she said. "I got tired of him but got very interested in the game."

"I'm glad," he said. She looked at him, and he added, "That you're so interested in the game, I mean. You're able to explain it to me so well."

"Of course," she said and went back to watching.

"This is your city. A park?"

"Yes," Bolan said, "Central Park. Perfect. Together, or separately?"

"Separately."

"It's just as well," Bolan said. "If these two got together, they'd probably kill each other."

They agreed on two different times for the meetings, later that evening.

"What are their names?" Ready asked.

"One is called Razor," Bolan said, "the other man's name is Armand Coles."

"Set it up with Razor first, and then Coles."

"As you wish," Bolan said. "Uh, I'll need the down payment we agreed on yesterday."

Ready took an envelope out of his jacket and slapped it down on the counter.

"The rest when the job is done," he said.

"As agreed," Bolan said, nodding.

Ready went to the door, flipped the sign back around and left.

Decker sat up and watched as Linda got dressed.

"Are you going to just look or get dressed?" she asked him.

He smiled and said, "I'll get dressed after you. I don't want to miss a single move."

"I said it before and I'll say it again," she said. "You're sweet."

There was not even a hint of the awkwardness that had been between them the night before.

Chapter Seventeen

Ready was an hour early for the meeting, and he took the time to study that area of the park. It was thick with foliage and trees, but there was a path, with benches along the way. It was quite beautiful and would probably be dangerous after dark.

Ready was sitting on the bench when a man approached. He was a stocky man, thick though the shoulders and chest and slightly bandylegged. From where he sat, Ready could see that the man did not wear a gun.

Then again, his name *was* Razor.

"You Ready?" the man asked him.

"I am," Ready said, hoping that he would hear none of the usual jokes about his name.

Apparently the man called Razor had no sense of humor.

"Bolan said you might have some work for me."

"I might if you're up to it."

"What's the job?"

"One man."

"I'm up to it."

"Did you know a man named Boil and his brother?"

"Second-raters," the man said. He was still standing, shifting his weight from one foot to the other.

"The man I want you to kill killed them."

"That's no recommendation."

New York defeated St. Louis soundly, 11-0—thanks to the masterful "pitching" by a fellow with the unlikely name of Hickey Daring, and the extraordinary "hitting" of another fellow named Matthews Boggs.

On the way back to her apartment, Decker said, "We could have a late lunch or an early dinner."

"I have to change."

"Would you like me to come back and pick you up?"

"No," she said. "You can come up and wait."

"All right."

Rosewood stopped in front, and Decker told him to wait.

"How long?"

"Just long enough for the lady to change," Decker said.

Rosewood gave Decker a sly look, which Decker ignored.

Upstairs Linda said, "I won't take long."

"That's all right," Decker said. "I'm sure you'll be well worth waiting for."

"You're sweet," she said. "Five minutes."

While he was waiting, Decker walked to the window and looked down at the back of the building. There was an alley, filled with debris but accessible.

"By the way," he called out, "we didn't decide. Shall we make it an early late lunch or an early dinner?"

He heard her come out. When he saw her, he stopped, stunned. She was indeed *well* worth waiting for.

She stood in the doorway, naked.

"How about a *late* dinner?" she asked.

* * *

"It's Bolan."

Bookman looked up at Largo from his lunch.

"As we suspected," he said.

"Yes," Largo said, "as *we* suspected."

"What did you find out?"

"Bolan's put out a call for Razor and Coles."

Bookman chewed thoughtfully on a bite of turkey sandwich.

"There's only one thing those boys do well," he said.

"Kill."

"Like you, my friend."

Largo shook his head. "Not like me."

"They're first-rate."

"But not in my class."

"Keep an eye on Decker."

"He says he doesn't need a baby sitter," Largo reminded Bookman.

"Make sure he doesn't know you're there, then," Bookman said. "You can do that, can't you, Largo?"

"I can do anything if you pay me enough, Bookman," Largo said.

"Good," Bookman said, "then go and do it."

It was exactly twenty-four hours since he'd been there last when Oakley Ready entered the junk shop.

Albert Bolan was behind the counter, as he had been the day before.

"The sign," he said, and Ready flipped the sign on the door over.

"What have you got for me?" Ready asked.

"Two men," Bolan said, "and they're not cheap."

"If they do their job."

"They'll do it."

"I want to meet them."

"Fine," Bolan said, "I'll set it up. Tell me where you're staying."

"No," Ready said, "I'll meet them somewhere in the open."

"Where?"

Ready shrugged.

"Maybe not," Ready said. "Bolan says you're one of the best."

"He's wrong," Razor said. "I am the best. Who's the man and where do I find him?"

"His name's Dover," Ready said and told Razor what hotel he was staying at. He still believed that Decker was Dover. "Bolan may be able to get you some more information about him."

"It would be nice if he had a lady," Razor said. He took a straight razor out of his pocket and said, "I like cutting their ladies . . . first."

Ready looked into the man's eyes and saw madness.

"I don't know if he has a lady," Ready said, "and I don't care. I just want the man killed."

"Why not kill him yourself?"

Ready didn't answer.

"Are you afraid of him?" Razor asked. He moved closer to Ready and waved his razor slowly in his face. "Do you scare easy, friend?"

Faster than Razor would have guessed, Ready grabbed the man's wrist, twisted it and forced Razor to his knees. He added a little more pressure, and the razor fell to the ground. From a folded newspaper on the bench, he took a two-shot derringer and pressed it against Razor's temple.

"All right, all right," Razor said, gasping at the pain in his wrist, "you can let go now. You proved your point."

"I should kill you," Ready said, cocking the gun.

"Then you *would* have to kill Dover yourself, wouldn't you?"

Ready decided not to tell Razor about Armand Coles. He released him and sat back on the bench. Razor retrieved his razor and stood up.

"When do you want this done?"

"As soon as possible."

"Do you care how it looks?"

"I don't care how you do it, as long as he looks dead when you're done."

"All right," Razor said. He put his straight razor away and rubbed his wrist. "All right. You'll know when it's been done. After that, you go and see Bolan and settle up."

"I'll be there."

Razor nodded, turned and left. Ready checked his watch and saw that he had half an hour before Armand Coles would arrive. He picked up part of the folded newspaper next to him on the bench, unfolded it and started to read.

Razor was a proud man—and a crazy one. Crazy, and angry. He rubbed his wrist as he walked through the park. He'd kill Dover, all right. But after Bolan had collected from Oakley Ready, he'd perform his next operation for free—on Ready!

As the second man came into view on the path, Ready folded the newspaper and put it down. He made sure the gun was out of sight beneath the folds.

"Are you the man I am to meet?"

Ready looked up at the man and said, "Are you Coles?"

"I am."

Coles spoke with a French accent. He was taller and more slender than Razor. If Ready didn't know better, he would have thought that Coles—certainly the more graceful of the two—was the man who killed with a blade.

"I'm Ready."

Coles sat down on the bench, apparently perfectly relaxed. The folded newspaper with the derringer was on the bench between them.

"What's the job?"

"I want a man named Dover killed," Ready said. He explained that "Dover" had killed Boil and his brother, and Coles had the same reaction to the news that Razor did. Then he told Coles what hotel Dover was in.

"I knew that."

Ready frowned.

"How?"

"I read the papers," Coles said. "I know what hotel Boil and his brother were killed in. The papers didn't say who killed them, however."

"Well, now you know."

Ready studied Coles. He was obviously more intelligent and less mad than Razor. Ready decided to tell him more than he had told the first killer.

"I've hired two of you, you know," Ready said.

"That would make sense. Who's the other?"

"Razor."

Coles made a face.

"What's the matter?"

"He's a barbarian, and he is crazy."

"So I gathered."

"Does he know about me?"

"No. I want you to watch Razor and let him try first. If he fails, then you go in."

"And if he succeeds?"

"Then I'll pay you both."

"And if Razor is killed and I succeed?"

Ready smiled. Coles was a man after his own heart.

"Then I'll pay you double."

Coles smiled and nodded.

"What's your weapon?" Ready asked.

"Oh," Coles said nonchalantly, "anything I find at hand—like this!"

Too late Ready realized what Coles was doing, and he was too slow to stop him. In a split second he was looking down the barrel of his own derringer.

"What was this for?" Coles asked.

"I was sure one of you would be crazy," Ready said.

"And you were right, weren't you?" Coles said.

"I was right," Ready said, but looking into Coles's eyes now, he wasn't sure which of the two men was crazier.

Coles took the derringer off cock and handed it back to Ready. The feverish glint in his eyes was gone as quickly as it had come.

"When do you want it done?" Coles asked.

"I told Razor as soon as possible. Will you know where to find him?"

"I'll find him," Coles said. "If he's too slow, I'll kill him, and then Dover."

As Coles stood up, Ready said, "I don't care how it works, as long as Dover ends up dead."

"Oh, he will," Armand Coles said. "He will."

Chapter Eighteen

"What are you doing in New York?" Linda asked.

"I told you before," Decker said. "I'm on vacation."

"Do you really expect me to believe that?"

He looked at her across the dinner table. They were dining in the same restaurant, at a more reasonable dinner hour. Linda was dressed more appropriately, in a lovely blue gown that left her shoulders bare. Decker felt almost inadequate in one of his new suits. He wished now he'd spent more of the Tyrone's money on clothes.

"Why not?"

She took a moment to put a piece of expertly prepared shrimp into her mouth.

"Most men who are on vacation would not react so . . . nonchalantly to being shot, the way you have. How is your shoulder, by the way?"

"It hurts a little . . . when I exert myself."

"Oh," she said, "next time you should let me do all the work."

He smiled and said, "Next time."

"Well?"

"Well what?"

"Are you going to tell me what you do that makes people want to shoot you?"

He stared at her for a few seconds and then said, "All right, I'll tell you."

"Good," she said, eating another piece of shrimp, "I'm all ears."

"No," he said, looking at her admiringly, "you are not."

"Don't change the subject."

He took a moment to eat a piece of steak. It was not as fine as some he'd had in the West—or in San Francisco—but it was very good.

"I told you the other night. I'm a bounty hunter. I hunt people."

"I'm not sure I understood you then," she said, putting her fork down. "You hunt them for . . . for money?"

"Everybody has to make a living," he said. "I hope you won't hold that against me."

"I don't know," she said. "Do you . . . kill them when you catch them?"

"I don't set out to," he said, "but some of them don't want to go peacefully."

"And then you kill them?"

"Your dinner is getting cold."

She looked down at her dinner and then back at him.

"That's what I am, Linda," he said. "A bounty hunter."

"And that's what you're doing in New York?" she said. "Hunting a man?"

"Yes."

"Why?"

"Because he's worth five thousand dollars."

"Is that the only reason?"

"No," Decker said after a moment, "he had a friend of mine killed. Shot in the back."

"Ah," she said, as if she suddenly understood.

"Don't do that," he said.

"What?"

"Don't think that you understand me so easily," he said. "Don't romanticize what I do. What I do I usually do for money and for no other reason."

"I see."

"I'm sorry if that disappoints you."

"It doesn't," she said, picking up her fork, "because I don't believe it."

"You don't."

"No," she said, spearing a piece of shrimp, "not for a minute. When you're ready to tell me the whole story, I'll listen."

"You're so sure there is more to the story?"

"Oh, yes," she said.

"Why?"

"Because I think I know you."

"After such a short time?" he said. "I wish I could say I know you so well."

"You will," she said. "You will."

Later, when they were together in her bed, he told her the whole story of how he had almost been hanged for a killing he didn't commit and how he decided to become a bounty hunter after that.

She listened quietly and intently and then hugged him to her when he was done.

"They almost hung you for nothing?" she asked, horror in her voice.

"Yes."

"That's horrible."

"Yes, it was," he said. "I was very young."

"I knew there was more to the story."

"Just a little."

"A little that explains a lot," she said, putting her head on his chest. He felt her tears wetting his skin.

He hugged her tightly to him, amazed that he'd wanted to tell her the rest of his story to her. As she fell asleep, he wondered if he wasn't losing sight of the real reason he'd come to New York.

He wasn't sure he cared.

Chapter Nineteen

Decker didn't hear the window open, but he heard a step on the windowsill. Linda was dead weight on his chest, and by the time he'd struggled out from beneath her, it was too late.

The man was on him, and a fist crashed into his face. He fell off the bed, reaching for the gun on the night table, but the man was there ahead of him and snatched it away.

"What's wrong—?" Linda said, coming awake.

"Quiet!" the man snapped. "Put on some light, girl!"

"Decker—"

"Do as he says," Decker said from the floor.

She leaned over and lighted the lamp on the night table on her side. In the yellow light that bathed the room, her naked body looked golden.

Decker looked at the man and saw him looking at Linda, licking his lips. Before he could react, however, the man had moved to Linda's side of the bed and had taken hold of her by the hair.

"She's a beauty, huh?" the man asked.

Decker, still sitting on the floor, didn't reply. The gun the man had taken from the table was not in his hand. Instead, he had a straight razor held against her throat. Her eyes were wide and fixed on Decker, but he could see that she had not panicked.

"I said she's a beauty, ain't she?" the man said again. Obviously he wanted an answer.

"Yes, she is."

"Yeah," the man said, licking his bottom lip. He moved his hand down from her neck to her breasts, where he pressed the blade against one of her nipples. "Real nice!"

"Decker—" she said, biting her lip.

"Why is she calling you Decker?" the man asked, looking puzzled. "Your name's Dover."

"No, my name's Decker."

"But—oh, I get it," the man said. "You're using a phony name."

"I'm using my real and only name," Decker said, "and it's Decker. Are you sure you've got the right man?"

"I've got the right girl," the man said, frowning. He leaned down so that his mouth was against Linda's ear and asked, "How many men you got, girl?" The man pressed his blade tightly against her nipple. A small drop of blood appeared, and she gasped. "That's what they like you to think, women," he said. "That you're the only one."

"You don't like women, do you?"

"I like them," the man said, "I like to cut their nipples off." He looked at Decker and added, "And I like to cut them while their men watch."

"Only I'm not her man."

"Ah," the man with the razor said, "now we're getting someplace. Dover's her man, right?"

"Right," Decker said, "and if he catches me here with her, he'll kill me."

"Is he coming here?"

"Yes."

"When?"

Decker shrugged, still trying to figure a way to his feet.

"When did you say he was coming, Linda?" Decker asked Linda, hoping that she wasn't too far gone to go along with the play. "It's nearly midnight now."

"He—he said he'd be here at one."

"See?" Decker said. "I'm running late already. He'll be here soon. I have to get out of here—" Decker said, starting to rise.

"You sit back down there on the floor, friend, or I'll cut her tit off," the man snapped.

Decker watched as he moved the razor from her nipple to the top slope of her right breast.

"I've done this before, you know," the man said. "You start here and just cut around." He made a circuit of her breast and then stopped at the upper slope again. "It comes right off in your hand," he said, sliding his other hand underneath to cup her breast. "I've cut off some big ones. These aren't too big, but they're nice and firm. Probably weigh as much as a small puppy."

"Well, like I told you," Decker said, standing up, "I'm not her man, so if you're going to cut off her breast I wish you'd wait until I leave. That's got to be messy."

Decker was standing now, in a much better position to mount an offensive.

The man with the razor was confused—it was plain on his face. He had one hand underneath her breast and one above, holding the razor. The gun he'd taken from the night table was in his pocket, and he didn't have one of his own.

"I'm getting dressed."

"Stop!"

He removed both hands from Linda's breast, and she sprawled onto the bed.

Now was the time for Decker to move, while the razor man was trying to get the gun from his pocket.

Decker launched himself over the bed and slammed into the man waist high. He felt the razor open his back as they fell to the floor. The razor man's hand was flailing away, trying to cut him again, while his other hand was pinned in his pocket, trying to get the gun out. His hand had closed around the gun, but there wasn't much he could do while they were both lying on it.

Decker knew this and knew he had to act fast. He set his left hand against the floor, lifted his weight up off the man and then swung his right fist in a short, vicious arc against the man's chin.

Decker then came down hard on the man's wrist to jar the razor loose, just in case he was playing possum. He turned him over to get his gun out. As he put his hand in the man's pocket, the man groaned and came awake, and his finger jerked the trigger. The gun was pointed at his own stomach. Decker felt the body jerk and then go limp.

He stood up and looked at Linda, who was sitting up in bed now.

"Are you all right?" he asked her.

"Y-yes," she said, "but you're not."

"What?"

"Your back," she said. "It's all full of blood."

Chapter Twenty

"You what?" Tally asked.

"Cut myself shaving."

"Very funny," the lieutenant said. "Where's the body?"

"What makes you think there's a body?"

"I can smell blood in the air," Tally said, "and from what I can see, a lot of it is yours."

"Can we get this man to the hospital?" Linda Hamilton asked irritably . . .

Decker had asked Linda if she knew anyone who would go for the police, and she said that the woman on the next floor up had a teenage son who had a crush on her. He'd go out if she asked him.

"Ask him," he'd said.

"You're bleeding—" she'd said, but he'd cut her off.

"Get him on his way, and then we can do something about that."

"All right."

"Where are your extra sheets?"

"In there," she'd said, pointing while dressing.

He took out a sheet while she was gone and covered the body of the razor man. When she returned, she took a pillowcase from a pillow and pressed it to the cut on his back.

"It's not as bad as I thought," she said. "All that blood fooled me. But you're still going to have to be sewn up."

"After the police arrive," he'd said. Now that they had, she wanted to get him taken care of . . .

"In a moment, Miss . . ."

"Hamilton."

"Miss Hamilton."

"The body's over there," Decker said, pointing to the lump beneath the sheet.

Tally walked over, lifted the sheet, took a look and then dropped it.

"You know him?" he asked Decker.

"No."

"But he tried to kill you."

"Yes."

"But you killed him first."

"By accident."

"Miss?"

Linda gave Tally a withering look before answering. She also pulled another pillowcase over and replaced the first one, which had soaked through with blood.

"We were asleep," she said, "and that man came through the window. He threatened to . . . to cut my—to cut me, and Decker jumped him. While they were struggling, Decker got cut, and then I heard a gun go off, and the other man was dead."

Tally looked at Decker.

"That's how it happened."

"I'm sure it did," Tally said as several other men entered the room. "Remove that one," he said, pointing to the body.

As they began to remove the body, Decker asked Tally, "Do you know who he is?"

"Of course," Tally said. "I know every killer and reprobate in New York."

"And which was this?"

"This was a definite killer," Tally said. "He was called Razor."

Decker flinched as Linda put more pressure on the wound and said, "I wonder why."

"Look at this," she said, looking at his shoulder. "You've started the other one bleeding, too. Lieutenant, we have to get him to the hospital."

"All right," Tally said. "Get up and get dressed. We can finish this there."

"All right," Decker said. When he stood up, the loss of blood suddenly took its toll. The next thing he knew he was falling down a dark well, and Linda was shouting his name . . .

Chapter Twenty-one

When he woke up, he saw Linda, dressed in her uniform.

When she saw he was awake, she came over to him and said, "That's right—this time we got you a bed."

"Are you all right?"

"I'm fine," she said, taking his wrist to take his pulse. "I'll be fine as long as we don't talk about it—"

"But—"

"—yet."

"Linda, I'm sorry—"

"Your back wounds have been seen to by a real doctor this time," she said, "and I'm on duty, so I'll have to leave you."

She started for the door, and he said, "But this was your day off."

"Was is right," she said. "Right now I think I need to work. Lieutenant Tally is outside. Shall I tell him that you're still asleep?"

"No, no," Decker said, "send him in."

"All right," she said and stepped out.

Decker wondered if he'd ever see her again. Hearing that he was a bounty hunter and accepting it was one thing but being personally involved in—and threatened because of—his profession was another thing entirely.

When the door opened again, Lieutenant Tally walked in.

"That's quite a girl," he said.

"Yeah," Decker said.

"Think she's scared off now?"

"The thought had crossed my mind, Lieutenant," Decker said. "Would you get me my clothes, please? I'm getting out of here."

"No, you're not."

"Yes, I am."

"Decker, play it smart for a change."

"Which means what?"

"If you had let me put a man on you, this might not have happened."

"Might not have," Decker said, coming down heavy on the *might*. "Just for your information, I took him alive. The idiot shot himself after I had him nice and subdued."

"I see."

"I could have found out who hired him."

"Could have," Tally said, coming down heavy on the *could*. "Maybe if you'd tell me who you're looking for—"

Decker shook his head.

"Does that mean you won't tell me or that you aren't looking for anyone?"

"Same difference."

"So you are looking for someone," Tally said. "I did some checking on you, Decker."

"That's so?"

"Yes."

"What did you find out?"

"That you've never taken a vacation in your life."

"I was due."

"I also found out that you're just about the best bounty man in the West."

"Hmm," Decker said, "I'd like to know who told you that?"

"Sorry," Tally said, "I was sworn to secrecy."

"I see."

"Must be a hell of a price to bring you all the way to New York."

"A price doesn't always explain everything, Lieutenant," Decker said. "Not even for a bounty man."

"Then maybe you want to tell me what the whole explanation is?"

Decker didn't reply.

"Decker, I can take Miss Hamilton down to my office and find out what you've told her. If I read you right, you've probably told her a lot more than you've told me."

"Don't do that," Decker said.

"One way or another," Tally said, "I want to find out what's going on."

Decker took a moment. Then he said, "All right." He told Tally what had happened to Dover in Harrison City.

"So you came in his place," Tally said, "and whoever killed him has been trying to have you killed, thinking you're him."

"Yes."

"And if he found out you weren't Dover?"

"It wouldn't make any difference," Decker said. "I still want him. I figure him not knowing Dover's dead gives me a small edge."

"And it's getting smaller by the minute," Tally said.

"Tell me about Razor," Decker said.

"What's to tell?"

"Is he for hire off the street, or would my man have had to make a contact?"

Tally's eyebrows went up.

"You are good, aren't you? You're quite right. Your man would have had to hire Razor through a contact."

"Like who?"

Rubbing his jaw, Tally turned and headed for the door.

"Like who, Tally?" Decker shouted.

"Get some rest," Tally said. "If you still want out in the morning, I'll come and get you."

"Tally!" Decker shouted, but the policeman went through the door and was gone.

Chapter Twenty-two

Ready's head snapped up when there was a knock at the door of his Delancey Street room. The only person who knew where he was the woman, and she was lying next to him.

"What—?" she began, but he put his hand over her mouth.

"Keep quiet!" he whispered in her ear, and she nodded.

He slipped out of bed and picked up his gun, then padded naked to the door. As the knock started again, he yanked the door open and thrust the gun straight out—into the stomach of Armand Coles.

"Oof!" Coles said. "Easy with that gun, *mon ami.*"

"What the hell are you doing here?"

"I apologize, but I followed you."

Ready reached out and grabbed Coles by the front of his jacket and yanked him into the room.

"Get in here!"

Coles staggered into the room, and Ready slammed the door behind him. He whirled on Coles then and pointed the gun at him.

"You'd better explain," he said to the French killer, but Coles was looking at the woman on the bed. He thought her face was rather plain, but he'd caught a glimpse of breast and thigh before she had covered herself completely with the sheet. She was very nicely padded and would be comfortable to lie with. Still, he could have gotten Ready a real beauty . . .

"It is very simple," Coles said. "I do not work in the blind."

"You work for Bolan."

"Ah, that is not quite true," Coles said. "I do work *through* Bolan on occasion, but I work *for* myself. Do you see the distinction?"

"I see it."

"Truly," Coles said, "you do not need that gun."

"That all depends on what you're doing here."

"Do you want the lady to hear?"

"Marcy, go in the other room."

"And do what?"

"Powder your nose—I don't care!"

Pouting, Marcy tossed the sheet back and stood up. She made no attempt to cover her nakedness now, as if getting back at Ready by letting Coles see all she had. Her breasts and buttocks reminded Coles of cannonballs. They barely jiggled as she flounced out of the room.

"My friend, next time you want a woman, let me know. I can get you one who will be fine in face *and* form."

"She's all right," Ready said. "Let me get some pants on."

Coles made an "after you" gesture with his hands and turned to find a seat. When he was seated in a straight-backed chair, Ready had a pair of trousers on and had tucked the gun into the front.

"Now, suppose you explain yourself," Ready said.

"Razor is dead."

"What happened?"

"He found Dover's woman, waited until they were

both asleep and then slipped into the room through a window."

"And?"

"And he must have gotten careless. Your man killed him."

"And what did you do?"

"Me?" Coles asked, smiling. "Why, I watched. The police came soon and took the body out. Later they took your man out and took him to the hospital. He seems to have a couple of wounds, one given him by Razor. He must have gotten the other from Boil and his brother."

"If he's hurt, then he's set up for you. What are you waiting for?"

"We need to renegotiate my price."

"What the hell are you talking about, renegotiate?"

"I'm not like our friend Razor, Mr. Ready. I don't go in to something blind and get myself killed."

"Talk plain."

"Razor didn't know who he was dealing with," Coles said. "I do."

"Dover," Ready said.

Coles shook his head.

"This man who killed Boil and his brother and Razor is not named Dover."

"Coles, what are you trying to pull—"

"Do you know a man called Decker?"

"I know of him. He's a man hunter, like Dover."

"He is a man hunter, but not like Dover," Coles said. "Decker is in a class all by himself."

"Wait a minute," Ready said. "Are you telling me that this man is Decker?"

"Yes, that's what I am saying."

"Decker!" Ready said as the truth sank in. "That

means Dover must have been killed in Harrison City. But why is Decker on my trail?"

"What more reason does a man need than five thousand dollars?"

Ready looked quickly at Coles, his hand hovering near his gun.

"Yes, I know what the price on you is. I have no desire to try and collect it. You see, I am wanted myself, though not quite as much as you. If I tried to collect your bounty, I would quickly be arrested. No, I have quite a different idea in mind."

"Keep talking."

"I want half your bounty if I kill Decker."

"Twenty-five hundred dollars?"

"Exactly."

That was less than half of what Ready was sitting on, but it was still a lot of money.

"You'll need help," Ready said. "Dover was good, but you're right about Decker. He's the best."

"I will not need help. I know New York, and Decker does not. That is all the edge I need."

Ready thought it over, biting his lip. At that point, Marcy came out of the other room and said, "Can I come back—"

"No! Stay out!" Ready shouted, and she backed quickly into the other room.

"Well?" Coles said.

"All right," Ready said after a moment, "all right. If you kill Decker, you've got it."

"Two thousand five hundred dollars?" Coles said. He wanted to make sure there were no mistakes.

"Yes, yes."

Coles smiled and stood up.

"Very well. I will let you know when it is done."

"Through Bolan."

"Forget Bolan," Coles said. "This is between you and me."

"How will I find you?"

"I will find you," Coles said. "Don't move from here. I will tell no one where you are."

It was against his better judgment to stay now that someone knew where he was, but Ready nodded and said, "All right, you'll find me here."

"Would you like me to arrange for another companion?" Coles asked, with a smile.

"No," Ready smiled, "no, this one is fine."

Coles wrinkled his nose and said, "She smells of cooking grease."

"She's a waitress."

"Ah," Coles said, nodding, "that explains it, then."

Ready watched as Coles walked to the door and left without another word. When the man was gone, he picked up a straight-backed chair and carried it to the door, where he jammed the back beneath the doorknob.

"Can I come out now?" Marcy asked from the other doorway, her tone contrite.

"Sure, honey, you can come out," Ready said.

"Who was that horrible man?" she asked, sliding back onto the bed.

"Just a business acquaintance, honey," Ready said, taking off his pants.

A business acquaintance he was going to have to kill.

Early the next morning Armand Coles was waiting outside Albert Bolan's junk shop when the man flipped his sign from CLOSED to OPEN and unlocked the door.

Coles entered, closed the door behind him and flipped the sign back to CLOSED.

"Coles," Bolan said from behind the counter. "What's going on?"

"Razor's dead."

"That's no concern of mine," Bolan said.

"No, I suppose it isn't. You'll just hire another killer and pay him in peanuts, right, Bolan?"

"What are you talking about?" Bolan asked, annoyed. "Get out. I've got a business to run. Come back when you've done the job Razor couldn't do."

"Bolan," Coles said, "I'm here to do a job I should have done a long time ago."

"What the hell—"

Coles took a straight razor from behind his back. "I'm making my own deals from now on," he said.

Chapter Twenty-three

When Decker awoke the next morning, he didn't know what ached more, his shoulder or his back. Also his mouth was very dry. As if on cue, a nurse entered.

"Good morning," she said.

"Where's Miss Hamilton?" he asked.

"She won't be on duty again until later tonight," this woman said. She came close to the bed, and he saw that she was a pleasant enough looking woman in her forties, certainly no Linda Hamilton.

She poured him some water from an iced pitcher and helped him drink it.

"I understand you'll be leaving us this morning."

"Is that so?"

"Mmm," she said. Apparently, she was the talkative type. "The doctor is very upset about it. He'd like to keep you here for a few days."

"Why is that?"

"He says a razor cut like that can get infected very easily." She looked down at him then and asked, "How on earth did you get a cut like that, anyway?"

"I cut myself shaving."

"I see," she said, frowning. "Well, I'll be back later to help you get dressed."

"Ah, will I be signing myself out this morning?" he asked as she headed for the door.

"From what I hear, there's a policeman coming to

get you," she said. She turned and said to him, "Do they arrest you now for cutting yourself shaving?"

She was out the door before he could figure out if she had a sense of humor or not.

When Tally came in two hours later, he was carrying Decker's clothes with him—as well as the gun and knife.

"Good morning," he said.

"It's about time," Decker said. "What took you so long to get here?"

"Sorry about that, but I started the day out in a particularly bad way."

"Oh?" Decker said, tossing back the sheet so he could swing his feet to the floor. "How's that?"

"With a murder."

"Anybody I know?"

"We were checking on contacts who might have supplied your man with Razor," Tally said.

"And?"

"And we found one of them dead. A man named Albert Bolan. I don't think we need look any further."

"How was he killed?"

"His throat was cut . . . with a straight razor."

Decker stood up and gingerly began to dress.

"So he was killed by Razor? That doesn't make sense if Razor worked for him."

"Well, he didn't actually work *for* him as much as *through* him. There are any number of miscreants who work through agents, so to speak. Bolan was an agent, but there's something else odd about his death."

"Like what?"

"He was killed this morning."

That stopped Decker again.

"But . . . Razor was dead this morning."

"Ah, yes," Tally said.

"Then somebody killed Bolan and wanted it to look like Razor did it."

"Go on."

"Somebody doesn't want to be found."

"Exactly."

"So we found the agent, but we're still in the blind."

"I'm afraid so," Tally said. "All we have now is one thing."

"Me?"

Tally nodded.

"You."

"You're putting me on the street so you can wait for whoever killed Bolan to try and kill me."

"That's such a crude way of putting it."

"But accurate."

"Yes," Tally said, "accurate."

"Well," Decker said, "if I'm to be your bait, the least you could do is help me with my pants."

The story of Albert Bolan's death was in the newspaper that morning. He was described as a store owner who was apparently killed during an attempted robbery.

Over breakfast at the small café where Marcy worked, Oakley Ready read the report.

Apparently, Armand Coles had cut his own deal in more ways than one.

The story had told Ready something else, as well.

Coles was treacherous, a man to be watched very carefully.

A man to be killed as soon as possible—as soon as Decker was dead.

Chapter Twenty-four

Tally took Decker to breakfast before returning him to his hotel. They went over to the small café where Decker had first eaten with Linda. The same waitress was there. She smiled at Decker but frowned at Tally.

"You want a clean cup today?" she asked.

"Madam," Tally said, graciously, "I apologize for my behavior the other day. Your cups are clean, your food is marvelous, and you, my dear, are a gem."

"Well," she said, mollified. "I'll get you your eggs, gentlemen."

As she walked away, Tally watched her.

"I didn't notice last time, but she is a remarkably well-put-together young lady."

"Maybe you should make this a regular eating spot," Decker said.

"Perhaps I will."

"All right, Tally," Decker said as they started on coffee, "what game are we playing today?"

"Just do what you've normally been doing. I'll have some men watching you."

"Not too obviously, I hope."

"My men are well trained, Decker," Tally said tightly.

Decker spread his hands and said, "I didn't mean anything, Lieutenant."

"Sorry," Tally said. "I'm sensitive about my men."

"If they're as good as you are, then I'm satisfied," Decker said.

"Jesus," Tally said, "spread it on any thicker and I'll have to get a shovel."

The waitress returned with their eggs, and Decker noticed that Tally had rated some extra today.

"Keep turning up the charm, Tally," Decker said, "and you'll be able to eat here for free."

"I am always charming, Decker," Tally said. "You've just been too busy to notice."

"Ah . . ."

After breakfast, Tally took Decker over to his hotel. They found Billy Rosewood waiting out front.

"I was gettin' worried," Rosewood said.

"I think it's about time you two became friends," Decker said. "Billy, Lieutenant Tally will explain what's happened. I think I'll go upstairs and get some rest."

"Good idea," Tally said, although Rosewood looked dubious.

As Decker entered the hotel, he heard Tally say, "Now, Billy, my boy . . ."

Turn on the old charm, Tally, he thought . . .

Decker collected his key from the desk clerk and made his way slowly to the second floor. He inserted the key in his lock and then stopped. He'd almost allowed his fatigue to allow him to become careless. He took out his gun and pushed the door slowly open.

There was somebody in the room, on the bed.

"I knew you were getting out today," Linda Hamilton said, sitting up. She was fully dressed, but she

was as pretty a sight at that moment as she would
have been naked.

Decker put the gun away and closed the door,
then started to take his coat off.

"Here, let me help you," she said, bounding to his
side.

"I didn't expect to see you again . . . for a while,"
he said.

"If you had asked me last night, I would have said
you'd never see me again," she said, putting his coat
on a chair.

"What changed your mind?"

"You did."

"How did I do that?"

"Just by being you," she said. She kissed him gen-
tly on the mouth and said, "Besides, I think you're
going to need a live-in nurse for a while."

"Is that so?"

"Yes," she said, unbuttoning his shirt, "that is so."

"Have you noticed how both wounds are on the left
side?" Decker asked later.

They were lying together in bed, she in the crook
of his right arm.

"And what does that mean?"

"It leaves my right arm free for you."

"And for your gun."

The remark hung in the air for a while.

"I'm sorry," she said finally.

"Don't be," he said. "I'm a lot better off because of
that."

"What are you going to do now?" she asked. "Keep
looking for that man?"

"Yes."

"He'll send someone else to kill you, won't he?"

"Most likely," he said. "That's what the police are counting on."

"The police?"

"Lieutenant Tally is putting some men on me, so you see, you don't have to worry."

"Why would I have to worry?" she asked. "I'll be right here with you."

"No," he said, "you won't."

"What are you talking about?"

"I think you had the right idea last night, Linda," Decker said. "Stay away from me . . . for a while. Let me and the police do what we have to do."

"Maybe they have to do it," she said, "because it's their job. You don't have to, though, Decker. You can let it alone."

"No, I can't."

"You mean you won't."

"Same thing."

"Is that what you really want?"

"What?"

"For me to stay away from you?"

"It's for your own safety."

"But is it what you really want?" she asked. "Not to see me for a while?"

Yes, he thought.

"No," he said.

Chapter Twenty-five

"Did you hear?" Bookman asked.

"I heard," Largo said. "It looks like one of Bolan's friends switched sides."

"Or went into business for himself."

"I guess he didn't inspire the same confidence you do."

"Don't pull my chain, Largo," Bookman said, putting down his knife and fork, "you'll ruin my meal."

"I didn't think that was possible."

"We both know that Bolan underpaid his people."

"Or downright cheated them."

"That's something you can't accuse me of," Bookman said, picking up his utensils again.

"You're right about that."

"Would you like a bite?" Bookman asked, indicating his breakfast.

"You'll excuse me for saying so, Bookman," Largo said. "I can work for you, but I don't think I'll ever be able to eat with you."

Bookman either didn't hear or ignored the remark.

"Largo?"

"Yeah?"

"Where were you while Decker was killing Razor?"

"I was outside the building."

"Doing what?"

"Watching."

"Why weren't you helping?"

"I didn't expect Decker to need my help," Largo said. "After all, it was only Razor he was dealing with."

"Did you see Coles in the area?"

"I didn't see him," Largo said, "but he was there."

"How do you know?"

Largo made a face and said, "I could smell him."

"I guess it's safe to assume that Coles killed Bolan."

"He never did have any . . . loyalty."

"Largo," Bookman said, "you're starting to worry me. Where is Decker now?"

"He's out of the hospital and in his hotel."

"Stay with him."

"He might have some extra help."

"Like who?"

"Police."

"Tally?"

"Yes."

"Tally will probably put somebody on him, whether he wants their help or not."

"I agree."

"Mmm, thank you so much."

Largo waited while Bookman chewed.

"All right, go and see him. Tell him I'm sorry I didn't get him the word on Bolan in time."

"I'm sure he'll appreciate that."

"And don't clash with the police. If they are there, they won't bother you. You are, after all, not known to them—thanks to me."

"I appreciate that, Bookman."

"Tell him about Coles."

"I will."

"Warn him that Armand is good."

"You want me to exaggerate, do you?"

"Just tell him, Largo."

"I will."

As Largo left, Bookman poured himself another cup of coffee. He hoped Decker wouldn't hold it against him that he hadn't gotten him the names in time. After all, things were happening very quickly.

Largo left and caught a cab to Decker's hotel. On the way he thought about Armand Coles's going into business for himself. He hadn't thought Coles was that intelligent.

Largo had worked for Bookman for three years now. Both Bookman and Largo knew that Largo was the best killer in New York, but Bookman was right. Thanks to him, nobody else knew, not the police, and not Armand Coles.

Maybe it was time, Largo thought, to make a move of his own.

Chapter Twenty-six

After much conversation, Decker finally convinced Linda that what he was suggesting was best.

"All right," she said. "I don't want you to get killed because you're worrying about me."

"That's as good a reason as any," he said, walking her to the door.

"Come and see me at the hospital?"

"I will."

"Promise?"

"I promise."

Decker kissed her and opened the door. Largo was standing there.

"Oh," Largo said. "I hope I'm not interrupting anything."

Linda looked worried, but Decker simply said, "I'll talk to you." She went out past Largo and walked down the hall. Largo watched her walk away until Decker said, "Are you going to stand out in the hall all day?"

Largo looked at him, then stepped into the room.

"What's Bookman want?"

"To apologize."

"About Razor?"

Largo nodded. "About not getting you the names in time."

"Which names?"

"Bolan, Razor . . . and Coles."

"Who is Coles?"

"Armand Coles," Largo said. "He's a killer who was sent in to back Razor up."

"He didn't do a very good job."

"I know Armand, Mr. Decker," Largo said. "He probably wanted you to kill Razor."

"Why?"

"Now he doesn't have to split the kill fee with anyone."

"That makes sense."

Largo saw the way Decker was moving.

"How hurt are you?"

"I'm a little stiff," Decker admitted.

"Does Tally have men on you?" Largo said.

"You tell me."

"There's one on the street and one in the lobby."

"What's your game, Largo?"

"I'll let you know when I decide," Largo said. "Right now I'm just working for Bookman, doing what he tells me to do."

"Which is?"

"Deliver a message, and keep an eye on you."

"Like you did last night?"

Largo smiled disarmingly.

"I knew you'd handle Razor. How did he cut you?"

"By accident."

"I figured it was something like that," Largo said. "Razor never saw the day he could handle someone of your caliber."

"Or yours?"

Largo shrugged.

"What about Armand Coles?"

"Ah," Largo said, "of late Coles has been surprising me a little."

"How's that?"

"He's been making smarter moves."

"Like killing Bolan?"

"Like going out on his own, yes."

"Tempted?"

"Like I said," Largo replied, "I'll let you know when I decide."

"Do you know where I can find Coles?"

Largo considered the question a moment. He was trying to decide whether he could, or should, answer.

"I think I might be able to tell you where he takes a drink or two," Largo finally said.

Afterward, Decker said, "And where will you be?"

Bookman's man—for now—walked to the door. He said, "I'll be around, Decker."

"I'll look for you."

"Don't," Largo said. "You won't find me."

"Hey," Decker said as Largo opened the door.

"What?"

"How do you know Coles drinks at this saloon?"

"Because," Largo said, "I drink there myself on occasion."

When Largo went in—and again when he came out—Tally's men studied him carefully. Neither of them had ever seen him before.

Later one of them would tell Tally that the man was "tall and slender, moved, well, like a killer. Only he was nobody we'd ever seen before."

"Sometimes those are the ones you should be most careful of," was Tally's reaction.

For now, Largo was seen as just another visitor to

the hotel. Tally's men went back to their normal procedure of surveillance.

Which meant they were half-asleep.

Decker got dressed and walked to the window of his hotel. It overlooked the street in front of the hotel, and Decker saw one of Tally's men standing in the doorway of a building across the way.

Decker decided that when he located Armand Coles, he didn't want the police around.

Not yet.

Chapter Twenty-seven

Decker kept a lookout on the front street, looking for Billy Rosewood. Finally he saw Rosewood's cab pull up. He hoped Billy would stay there long enough for him to get down there.

Decker put the little .32 in his pocket and then picked up his sawed-off shotgun. It was about time his old friend went along with him. The next time somebody tried to take a piece out of him, that somebody was going to end up in pieces—after Decker questioned him. He tucked the shotgun inside his coat and left the room.

Decker went downstairs and found Rosewood leaning against the cab.

"I wondered if you died up there," Rosewood said.

"What made you come back?"

"Cap'n," Rosewood said, "you don't strike me as the type to let a little bullet and razor keep you from doing what's got to be done."

"Good man," Decker said. "There's a policeman across the street."

"Yep," Rosewood said, "and one in the lobby."

"I want to lose both of them."

"Well, hop in and let's get it done."

Decker got into the cab, and Rosewood climbed up top and got it moving.

Looking out the back, Decker saw the two policeman scramble into a cab of their own. Soon it was

clear that their driver was not as skillful as Rosewood or as knowledgable about the city's side streets.
In a matter of minutes, Rosewood had lost them.

"Where to now, Cap'n?" he shouted down.

"A reliable gunsmith," Decker shouted back.

"Sit tight," Rosewood said, "be there in a couple
of minutes."

Julian's Gun Shop was a hole in the wall off the Hud-
son River. Rosewood stopped the cab and jumped
down, opening the door for Decker.

"I suspect you want something special," he said.

"You suspect right. Is this fella any good?"

"Are you kidding? Even the police come here for
their special items. What do you want done?"

Decker took his shotgun out of the cab.

"That little gun of yours is fine, Billy, but I think I
need my own weapon along from now on."

"Gonna ruin the lines of that nice new jacket."

"I thought you said he was good."

Rosewood shrugged and said, "He's good, but he
ain't no tailor."

Rosewood led the way into the shop. Behind the
counter was the tallest man Decker had ever seen.
Painfully thin, he had black hair that came to a
widow's peak. Even though it was only 11:00 a.m.,
he had a five o'clock shadow.

"Lee," Rosewood said, "this here's a friend of
mine. His name is Decker."

"Decker," Lee said, nodding his head. "Seems I've
heard that name somewhere."

Decker wondered where. Tally had done his job
keeping Decker's name out of the newspapers so
that Ready would think Dover was still after him.

"I thought the name of this place was Julian's?" Decker asked.

"It is," Lee said. "I'm Lee Christopher. My brother's name is Julian. He started this job, and I took it over when he died."

"I see."

"Decker," Lee Christopher said, still chewing the name over. "Yeah, I've heard your name before. Well, it'll come to me. What can I do for you?"

"I want to carry this," Decker said, putting his shotgun on the counter, "without anyone knowing."

"You could use a smaller gun," Lee said.

"We been through that, Lee," Rosewood said. "The man knows what he wants."

"OK," Christopher said, picking it up. "Let's see what we got. You want to use that jacket?"

"Yes."

"Let me have it."

Decker took the coat off, moving gingerly.

"Looks like you've had some trouble already."

"Some," Decker said, handing over the coat.

"Well," Christopher said, holding the coat up, "it would help if you were some heavier, but I can rig a holster on the inside of this jacket—not a full holster, mind you. Wait a minute. I know what I can do—here." He looked at Decker and asked, "How much time have I got?"

"We need it yesterday," Rosewood said.

"Are you paying?"

"Yes," Decker said.

"Come back in an hour. I'll be closed, but bang on the door."

"Thanks," Decker said, but the man didn't hear, already lost in deep thought.

"Come on," Rosewood said, "I know where we can get a drink while we're waiting."

Decker and Rosewood left the shop and walked to a nearby saloon. Decker took a table, and Rosewood got two beers from the bar and joined him.

"Once you've got your jacket rigged, where are we headin'?" he asked Decker.

"The Bowery."

"What the hell for?"

"You know a place called the Bucket of Blood?"

"Know it?" Rosewood said. "Cap'n, even I stay clear of that place."

"Well, that's where I want to go."

"Why?"

"Because the next guy who's going to try to kill me drinks there."

"And that's a reason to go?" Rosewood asked. Then he held his hands up and said, "Wait, I know—that's the best reason to go."

"Right. This time I don't want to wait for him to find me. I want to find him."

"I suppose from your point of view, that's the way to do it."

"And from yours?"

"I believe I'd give serious thought to finding a new city to live in."

"Billy, if you don't want to go—"

"No, no, I'll take you, Cap'n. You're the one paying the freight."

"That reminds me," Decker said. "I owe you money—"

Rosewood raised his hand and said, "We got time to settle up later."

"You're an optimist."

"Well, if you get killed at the Bucket, I believe I'll be in too much trouble with Tally to spend any money—that is, if I ain't dead, too."

"You won't be," Decker said. "You're just going to drop me off. You aren't coming in."

"You got eyes in back of your head?"

"What's that mean?"

"In that place two eyes aint' nearly enough, and even four is like to make you go cross-eyed, but four's all we got between us, and we might as well use them all."

"You'll need this, then," Decker said. He took the .32 out of his pocket and passed it to Rosewood under the table.

"I had a feeling this thing was gonna be coming back to me sooner or later," Rosewood said, putting it in his pocket. "I think I would rather it was later."

Chapter Twenty-eight

Largo had followed Decker to Julian's Gun Shop, which he knew well. He also used Lee Christopher for special work. Christopher knew Largo by sight but did not know his name or that he worked for Bookman.

One of Bookman's hard and fast rules when he agreed to take Largo on was that anonymity be maintained. It was only lately that Largo had begun to chafe beneath that cloak.

Maybe Decker's search for a man named Ready, and Armand Coles's involvement, would be the setup Largo needed to cast off that cloak.

Maybe.

They each had another beer. Then they walked over to Julian's Gun Shop.

"Why doesn't he change the name?" Decker asked.

"If your brother started the business, would you change the name?"

"I see your point."

When they got to the shop, the front door was locked, as Christopher had said it would be. Rosewood banged on it for a while, until the tall man came and opened it.

"Come in, come in," Christopher said. He seemed to be very excited about something.

"Did you come up with something?" Decker asked.

"Did I!" Christopher said. "Come and see."

They followed Lee Christopher into his workshop. The walls were covered with all kinds of guns, as well as some other weapons.

"Quite a collection," Decker said, eyeing a curved saber hanging on the wall.

"Thank you," Christopher said. "I'm quite proud of it. Here, here is your jacket. Try it on."

Decker let the man help him on with the coat.

"Now, look inside, on the left side."

"Why the left side?" Decker asked. "I'm right-handed. I guess I should have told you that."

"I saw that when you gave me the gun," Christopher said. "It doesn't matter. Look."

Decker looked inside at the back of the coat. He saw not a holster but two bands that were closed.

"They're light," he said.

"Clamshell," Christopher said. "Strong but light. And they're on hinges."

"Hinges?" Decker asked. "What for?"

"Watch."

Christopher picked up Decker's shotgun. As Decker held the coat open, he swung the bands open on their hinges, fitted the shotgun into the place, then snapped them back into place. The shotgun was now fitted snugly into the bands.

"Not so light now," Decker said.

"Keeping it from being seen is going to be your problem. If you keep your arm over it and keep the weight from hanging, you should be all right."

"How do I get it out when I want it?"

"That's the beauty of this. Let the jacket go."

Decker let it go, and it closed. It hung badly from

the weight of the gun, but if he kept his hand in the pocket, he could keep the weight under control.

"Now reach for it with your right hand," Christopher said, his eyes shining.

Decker reached for the shotgun, and as his hand closed over it, the two bands snapped open and the shotgun came free in his hand.

"You see?" Christopher said, a look of glee on his face.

Decker stared at the tall gunsmith, then fit the shotgun back into place and snapped the bands closed. When he went for the gun this time, he did so faster. The hinges snapped the bands back, and the shotgun seemed to leap free.

"You see how much easier it is for you to get it by reaching across to the left side?" Christopher asked.

"Yes," Decker said, "even faster than if it was on my hip."

He put the gun back in place and snapped the hinges shut.

"That's amazing," he said.

"That's fast," Rosewood said.

"The hinges snapped open as soon as you touch the gun, putting the slightest pressure on them, and yet they won't open accidentally. I can practically guarantee that."

Decker put the shotgun back in place and faced Christopher.

"I can see you're as good as Billy said you were."

"It's just something I've been toying with," the man said, looking embarrassed. "You've given me the chance to put it into practice."

"How much do I owe you?"

Christopher quoted a price that surprised Decker. "That's too cheap."

"As I said," the tall man said, "you've given me a chance to put something into practice. That's more valuable to me than money."

Decker looked at Rosewood for a sign as to whether or not he should argue, and Rosewood shook his head.

Decker paid Christopher what he asked.

"Thank you," the tall man said.

"I should thank you."

"I don't think so," the other man said.

"Why?"

"Because that rig will probably get you killed."

"Why do you say that?"

"It's obvious to me you need that gun because you're going into a nest of vipers."

"So why will I end up getting killed?"

"Because it's been my experience with vipers," Christopher said, "that one of them will usually take a bite out of you."

"I'll let you know what happens."

"I'll probably read about it in the newspapers."

"Either way," Decker agreed, "you probably will."

When Decker and Rosewood came out of the gun shop, Largo was across the street, out of sight. His sharp eye picked up the heavy hang of Decker's jacket immediately.

Decker appeared ready to go and have a drink at the Bucket of Blood.

Chapter Twenty-nine

"This is your last chance to change your mind."

Rosewood had stopped the cab down the street from the Bucket of Blood, and he and Decker had walked to the door.

"You make this sound like the gate to hell, Billy," Decker said. "How much worse could this be than some of the places I've been to on the Barbary Coast?"

"In San Francisco they just shanghai you," Rosewood said. "Here they kill you."

"Let's go inside."

"One final word of warning."

"What?"

"You're not a regular," Rosewood said. "Leave the women alone, no matter how hard they try."

"How hard is that going to be?"

"Hard," Rosewood said, "believe me—but do it without insulting them. Even the women in here carry knives."

"Jesus," Decker said and opened the door.

The first thing that hit him was the smoke. It was thick, most of it floating close to the ceiling, with tendrils of it coming down here and there because it had nowhere else to go.

After that, it was the heat. Not exactly oppressive, it was the kind of heat given off by many bodies in a small space—not that the Bucket of Blood was small, but it was doing a land-office business at this time of day.

If Armand Coles *was* in here—and even if Decker knew what he looked like—it would be almost impossible to find him.

Decker had to hope that seeing him in one of his own drinking places would push Coles's timetable up, make him move before he was ready.

Decker entered first and went to find a spot at the bar. He had a beer in his hand when Rosewood came in a few minutes later. Decker had to give the younger man credit. If he was scared, he certainly didn't show it. He found a spot down the bar from Decker and ordered a beer.

Looking around, Decker saw that Rosewood had been right about the women. They were all young and provocatively dressed, so that much of their breasts were showing—and they all had big breasts. It seemed to be a requirement for the job.

Decker knew he was drawing curious glances—from the bartender and several of the patrons—but he ignored them and looked around the room, occasionally sipping his beer. He figured that the clientele here knew a strange face could always be law, and he figured they were all trying to decide about him.

Rosewood was not drawing as much attention as Decker was. Either Billy Boy had been here before, or he simply didn't present the aura of physical danger Decker did.

Decker had been there about ten minutes when one of the women gave him a try. Actually it wasn't her idea. She had been sitting on a man's lap when he leaned over and whispered in her ear. She looked up at the bar, saw Decker, then nodded and got out of the man's lap.

The man was a big fella with a potbelly and a heavy beard. He could have been Bookman's brother, but there was no food grease in his beard. Also he hadn't nearly as much hair on his head as he had on his face, and his nose was bigger and redder than Bookman's. Where Bookman's vice was food, this man's obviously was whiskey.

The girl was a real beauty. She had long dark hair, hoop earrings, a wide mouth painted thickly red. She was wearing a blouse that fell way off her shoulders, so that the upper slopes and a lot of cleavage showed. She had large, firm, pear-shaped breasts, and Decker found himself wondering what was holding the blouse up.

"Hello, stranger," she said, moving in close to him.

"Hello."

She pressed right up against him, so that he could feel the heat of her and the pressure not only of her breasts but of her large nipples, which were hard. Her perfume was thick and heady and hung around her like a cloud.

"You're new here."

"Yes, I am."

"My name is Lola."

"Hello, Lola."

"Don't you have a name?"

"I do," Decker said, "but I don't give it out at the drop of a hat."

She pouted, pushing out her lush lower lip. She was so close he could bite it, and was sorely tempted to do so.

"You're not very friendly."

"I'm sorry," he said. "I have other things on my mind."

"You're not a lawman, are you?"

"No, honey, I'm not a lawman."

"That's good," she said, "because this bunch would have you for lunch if you were."

"From the looks of them," Decker said, "they might, anyway."

"Not if you're nice to me," she said. She shifted around so she could press herself flat against him and, in doing so, came into contact with the shotgun.

"Whoa," she said. "Mister, you're looking for trouble."

"Who's the man who sent you over here?"

Without turning to look at the bearded man, she said, "His name is Mosca. The others called him King Mosca."

"What'd he want to know?"

"Your name."

"He also wanted to see how I'd react if you pressed your gorgeous body up against me, right?"

"You're pretty smart," she said. Then she licked her lips and asked, "Do you really think I'm gorgeous?"

"Absolutely."

"You're nice," she said. "It's too bad Mosca's gonna kill you."

"No, he's not," Decker said. "You go back and tell Mosca I'd like to talk to him."

"About what?"

"That's between him and me, Lola. Just go and tell him, all right?"

"What's in it for me?"

Decker took some money out of his pocket and pushed the bills down between her breasts. The valley there was warm and sweaty.

"I'll tell him."

"By the way," he said, grabbing her elbow.

"What?"

"You wear too much perfume," he said. "You don't need it. You'd smell fine without it."

"All sweaty?" she said, looking at him like he was crazy.

He smiled and said, "Especially all sweaty."

"Mister," she said, "if Mosca doesn't have you for lunch, I just might."

She went back to Mosca's table, sat in the big man's lap and gave him Decker's message. Mosca looked past her, studying Decker. The big man had three other men sitting with him, and Decker felt sure that if all three stood up right now, Lee Christopher's contraption was going to get an instant try out.

From where Decker stood, Mosca's eyes looked black, like two holes in his face. They were expressionless as he studied Decker. Then the big man said something to Lola and squeezed her ass. She got up and walked over to Decker.

"Mosca's interested in you," she said.

"Good."

"So am I."

He smiled and said, "Even better."

"First Mosca, then me. Right?"

"Right."

"All right," she said. She took his hand and said, "Come with me."

As she led him to Mosca's table, Decker sneaked a glance over at Rosewood, who looked at Decker and then at the ceiling, as if to say, "Now you went and did it!"

Chapter Thirty

"You wouldn't tell Lola your name," Mosca said.

"There wasn't any reason to."

"Will you tell me?"

"Are you inviting me to sit with you?"

"Yes."

"Then I'll tell you my name."

Decker had been thinking about this as he crossed the floor to Mosca's table. If he told the truth and said his name was Decker, would that dissuade Armand Coles from coming after him? Should he lie and say his name was Dover?

No. He decided that the time for playing someone else was past. Let Coles and everybody else know whom they were coming after.

"My name's Decker."

"All right, Mr. Decker," Mosca said. "Have a seat."

Now, there were only four chairs at the table, and all of them were taken. Lola was sitting on Mosca's lap again.

Decker looked around, and there were no chairs available to be pulled over from another table.

"Doesn't seem to be a chair," he said to Mosca.

"Pick one," Mosca said, indicating the other three occupied chairs at his table.

Decker looked at all three seated men, each of whom looked more than willing to die for the chair he was sitting in—if Mosca gave the word.

"They're your men," Decker said. "You pick the one you want to die over a chair."

Mosca stared at Decker for a few moments, then looked at one of his men and said, "Get up, Sykes."

The man named Sykes got up, and Decker sat down.

"Why do you have a shotgun inside your jacket?" Mosca asked.

"I heard this was a rough place."

"And is it?"

"Not so far."

Mosca laughed, a great booming laugh that drew everyone's attention.

"You don't think this is a tough place, huh?"

"I said not so far."

"There ain't a man in here who wouldn't kill you if I gave the word."

"That might be so," Decker said, "but you let me get close enough so that if you did, you'd be the first to die. That tells me that you aren't about to give the word."

Mosca's black eyes studied Decker, and then he said, "You're right about that. Why don't you tell me what you're doing here, Decker?"

"I'm looking for a man."

"Do you see him here?"

"I don't know," Decker said. "I don't know what he looks like."

"You've never met him?"

"No."

"Then why the hell are you looking for him?"

"He's going to try and kill me."

"He is?" Mosca said, raising his bushy black eyebrows. "Now, why would he want to do that?"

"He's being paid to."

"By who?"

"By another man."

"Well," Mosca said, "that sure makes sense. It's a better reason than some of these rats need."

"His name's Coles."

"Whose name?"

"The man I'm looking for," Decker said. "Armand Coles."

"The man who's gonna kill you?"

"That's right. He drinks here sometimes."

"That a fact?" Mosca said. "What's the other man's name? The one that done the hiring?"

"That's not your concern."

That was the first thing that Decker had said that seemed to upset Mosca. The big man leaned forward, causing Lola to fall off his lap and land with a thud on the floor.

"Jesus, Mosca—"

"Shut up and take a walk!" Mosca growled at her.

She got to her feet, rubbing her ample posterior, and walked over to the bar.

"You come in here," Mosca said to Decker, leaning on the table, "where you don't belong, and you tell me something ain't my concern?"

"That's what I said."

"You got a lot of guts."

"Do you know Coles?"

"Everybody knows Coles," Mosca said, "but nobody here knows you."

"What's that mean?"

"That means that if Coles was in here, and he made a move against you, he'd have a lot of backing, and you'd have none."

"Guess that makes me kind of foolish, don't it?" Decker said.

"Guess it does."

"So I guess I'll be leaving."

"If I say so, you will."

"If I don't," Decker said, "you don't."

Mosca sat back in his chair and folded his hands over his belly.

"I said I knew Coles, not that I was ready to die for him. You can leave—just don't come back."

"I won't."

"And take your pup over there at the bar with you."

Decker looked at Billy Rosewood and jerked his head toward the door. Rosewood moved away from the bar, walked to the door and left the saloon.

"Now you."

"If you make a move against me, Mosca, I'll have to kill you."

"This is between you and Coles, Decker," Mosca said. "I said we knew him, but Armand Coles has no friends in here."

"Good enough," Decker said.

Decker stood up, then looked over at Lola, who was leaning on the bar with both elbows, her impressive chest thrust forward.

"Maybe another time, Lola."

She smiled at him and winked, and Decker backed toward the door, deeping his eyes on Mosca. At the big man's slightest move, he would pull his shotgun and blow the man's gut wide open—although he'd prefer to avoid that.

He stopped when his back hit the door.

"If Coles is here," he said out loud, "or if any of you ever see him, tell him to come at me from the front and not from the back like a coward. You tell him that."

Decker reached behind him with his left hand, opened the door and backed out.

"Whew!" Billy Rosewood said. "I thought for sure we were dead."

"Now, what made you think that?"

"The way Mosca was talking."

"Billy," Decker said, "talking doesn't kill. Killing kills."

"What does that mean?"

"That means that if a man's going to kill you, he doesn't talk about it—he does it."

"You said you'd kill Mosca."

"The call was his," Decker said, "but believe me, if he had made it, I would have killed him."

"I believe you."

"Let's get going," Decker said. He started down the street to where Rosewood had left his cab.

"Where to?" Rosewood asked, trotting to catch up.

"The hospital."

"You hurt?"

"No," Decker said, "I'm just keeping a promise."

Chapter Thirty-one

Linda had told Decker that she'd be working day shifts that week, so he knew he'd find her there.

"Want me to wait?" Rosewood asked.

Decker considered cutting Billy Rosewood loose for good but thought better of it. He still might need him to show him around.

Decker gave Rosewood some money and said, "Come back after your dinner."

Decker went into the hospital. As the front-desk nurse told him where Linda was working, he saw her waving to him from the end of the hall.

She rushed down the hall and took his arm.

"Where should we go for dinner?"

"That same restaurant. Where we first ate together."

"I didn't know you were so sentimental."

"I didn't, either."

They walked to the small restaurant and were seated by a different waitress.

"Where's Marcy?" Linda asked.

"You're Linda?" the girl asked.

"Yes."

"Marcy said to tell you that you might have switched shifts, but she couldn't. She's still working eight p.m. until four a.m."

"Tell her I'm sorry for her," Linda said, and the two women laughed together.

They ordered lunch, and then Linda leaned forward and said, "What did you do this morning?"

"I bearded a nest of vipers."

"And?"

"And I got out without being bitten."

"Is that unusual?"

"So I'm told."

"How are you feeling?"

"A bit stiff."

"Maybe you should come back with me and let me check your dressings."

"No, they're fine. I checked them this morning."

"You're just afraid that once we get you in there, we won't let you out."

"That's exactly what I'm afraid of. I've never liked doctors much, and these have been my first experiences with hospitals."

"You've never been to a hospital before?"

"Just military field hospitals, but they're quite different."

"How?"

"Most of the people there are dead."

The waitress came with their dinner, and they ate, engaging in small talk—tiptoeing around what they were both thinking about.

Over coffee, Linda decided to be more direct.

"Have you thought of giving this all up and leaving?"

"Do you want me to leave?"

"That's not my question."

"What is?"

"You know what the question is. You're just avoiding the answer."

"No. *You're* avoiding the answer, because it's not the one you want to hear."

She paused as the waitress came over with their coffee.

"You're very frustrating."

"I know."

"If you did leave . . ."

"What?"

"If you did leave . . . I'd be willing to go with you . . . if you asked."

Decker didn't reply.

"Not that I'm hinting, mind you," she said, "but I just thought you might—" She stopped and looked at the ceiling. "I swore I wouldn't make a fool of myself."

"You haven't."

"Yes, I have."

"No," Decker said. "You mentioned something I've been thinking a lot about."

"Only you haven't made up your mind yet?"

"No, I haven't."

"Well, that's all right," she said. "When you do, though, you'll let me know, won't you?"

"You'll be the first."

Rosewood was waiting when Decker and Linda returned from dinner.

"There's your sidekick," she said, waving to Rosewood. He waved back. "He likes you a lot, you know."

"Really?"

"In fact, he might even idolize you."

"I'll break him of that."

"And what about me?" she asked. "Will you break me of . . . of you?"

"I hope not," he said, leaning over to kiss her cheek. She moved her head so that he kissed her lips instead. He didn't complain.

"Come and see me," she said.

"Here at the hospital?"

"Where it's safe."

"For you," he said, and she smiled and went in.

Decker walked over to where Rosewood was waiting.

"She's a nice lady," Rosewood said.

"Yes, she is."

"And pretty."

"Very pretty."

"When you leave New York, are you going to ask her to go with you?"

"I haven't decided yet, Billy," Decker said, "but when I do, you'll be the second to know."

"Who'll be the first?"

Decker looked at Rosewood, who blushed.

"Oh, of course," he said. "That makes sense."

Chapter Thirty-two

Largo was impressed with Decker. He didn't want to be, but he was.

He had been sitting in the back of the room when Decker entered the Bucket of Blood. He knew there'd be no danger of Decker seeing him. He just sat back and watched Decker go to work.

After Decker left the place, Largo sat back, shaking his head. He'd never seen anyone talk to Mosca like that. Mosca was small time—a large fish in a small pond—but the Bucket of Blood was *his* place, filled with *his* people, and he had allowed Decker to walk out. That was a tribute to Decker's ability to intimidate.

Largo left the Bucket of Blood shortly after Decker. Armand Coles was not there, but word would get back to the Frenchman that Decker had called him a coward. Coles would feel that he had to retaliate because of this insult to his pride.

Largo was different from Coles. He had pride, but he tempered it with a cool head. Decker, he knew, was trying to force Armand Coles into going after him before he was ready.

And he would succeed, too.

The question was, would Decker survive?

The two men sat across from each other in a small café, drinking coffee.

"Why did we meet here?" Coles asked.

"I like it here," Oakley Ready said.

Coles eyed the firm calves of the waitress who had just served them.

"Uh-huh, I see."

"Now you tell me why we had to meet at all," Ready asked.

"It's about your friend Decker."

"He's not my friend," Ready said. "I've never even met him. What about Decker?"

"I'm going to kill him."

"Well, hell, that's what I'm paying you for."

"I need an edge."

"I thought you were good."

"I'm alive," Coles said. "In my business, that means I'm good. It also means I sometimes keep an edge."

"What makes you need an edge this time?"

"Decker challenged me."

"You spoke to him?"

"Uh, no. He sent me a message."

"Where?"

"At a saloon where I drink."

"He knew your name."

"Yes."

"How?"

"I don't know."

"What do you want to do now?" Ready said.

"I'm going to accept his challenge."

"But you need an edge."

Coles nodded.

"All right," Ready said, "I think I have an idea . . ."

"Where are we going tomorrow?" Rosewood asked.

"I haven't the faintest idea."

They were in Decker's room at the hotel.

"You just gonna wait for Coles to come after you?"

"I don't think I have long to wait, do you?" Decker said. "I just have to make myself visible."

"So you want to ride around tomorrow?"

"Maybe walk around."

"That wouldn't be smart, would it?" Rosewood asked. "I mean, he could pick you off from a rooftop with a rifle, couldn't he?"

"He could," Decker said, "but he won't."

"What makes you say that?"

"Because I challenged him, in the Bucket of Blood," Decker said. "I called him a coward. He's going to have to come right at me, Billy. Right straight at me, just to prove he's better than I am."

"And is he?"

"Well, we don't know that, do we?"

"What if he is?"

"If he is better," Decker said, "then I'll have to hope I'm luckier."

"That's a helluva attitude."

A knock on the door stopped Decker's reply. He rose and opened the door and Lieutenant Tally walked in.

"Get lost, Billy," Tally said.

"Nice to see you, too, Lieutenant," Billy said, getting up and walking toward the door. "Tomorrow morning, Decker?"

"See you then, Billy."

Rosewood left and closed the door behind him.

"You lost my men today."

"Did I? I'll help you find them."

"You know what I mean!"

"Tally, I can't be responsible if your men weren't able to keep up with me."

"Oh, that's all right," Tally said, waving a hand. "We managed to pick you up again later."

"You did?"

"What were you doing at the Bucket of Blood?"

"Having a drink with some friends?"

"Sure," Tally said. "Those are the kind of friends you make when you've only been in New York for a few days, right?"

"How did you know I was there?"

"I have a couple of men watching the place. They saw you."

"Why did you have someone watching the place?" Decker asked. He wondered how Tally had found out about Armand Coles.

"I always have a couple of men watching that place, Decker."

From everything Rosewood had told Decker about the Bucket of Blood, that made sense.

"What were you looking for there?" Tally asked. "Or should I ask who?"

"Billy told me about the place. I was curious."

"Mmm-hmm," Tally said, walking around the room. He reached for the straight-backed chair where Decker had hung his coat. He picked up the coat.

"My men were right."

"About what?"

"About your jacket hanging pretty heavy," Tally said, hefting the coat in his left hand. With his right he held it open. "Very heavy, I see."

"I felt I needed to carry around a little more fire-power."

"Yes, well, if you're going to visit places like the Bucket of Blood, I agree." Tally replaced the coat.

"Decker, I can't protect you if you're going to run away from me."

"If I have your men around me, Tally, no one's ever going to make a move," Decker said. "I don't intend to spend the rest of my life in New York."

Tally walked toward the door and said, "If you keep playing it your own way, you just might end up doing that—spending the rest of your very *short* life here."

When Linda Hamilton left the hospital to go home, she didn't notice the man who was following her. She was thinking about Decker and whether he would ask her to leave New York with him.

The man followed her all the way home. Then, as she was fitting her key into the lock of the front door of her building, he closed the distance between them and stepped into the doorway behind her.

"Wha—?" she said, alarmed.

"Take it easy," the man said. "Go ahead, open the door."

"Who are you?"

"Quiet," he said. After she opened the door, he said, "Let's go upstairs."

They went up, and she opened the door to her apartment.

"Inside," he said, pushing her. "Light a lamp."

She did as she was told.

"Oh, I can see what Decker sees in you, Miss Hamilton," the man said. "You've very beautiful."

"What now?" she asked, standing awkwardly in the center of the room.

"Now," he said, "we wait."

Chapter Thirty-three

In the morning, Decker had breakfast with Rosewood.

"They're following us again," Rosewood said when they were seated in that small, nameless café Decker had come to like so well.

"I know."

"What did Tally say last night?"

"That he didn't want me to get killed."

"That's nice of him," Rosewood said. "Do we lose them again?"

"I don't know yet," Decker said. "Why don't we do a little sightseeing today?"

"Why not?" Rosewood said. "You're paying the freight."

"Let's go . . ."

The day went by uneventfully. They went to Central Park and walked; they went to museums and walked; they went to different neighborhoods that Rosewood thought Decker might find interesting—and walked.

"You've been walking around all day with a target painted on your back, and nobody's so much as looked at it twice. How many more days do you think you can do this?"

"I don't know."

"*I'm* a nervous wreck."

Decker smiled.

"Wait here. You can drive us to dinner."

When Decker went into the hospital to get Linda for dinner, he found out she hadn't come to work that night.

"Did she send word why?"

"No," the nurse at the desk said. "And that's not like her, at all."

"No, it isn't," Decker said.

He hurried out to Rosewood's cab.

"Where is she?" Rosewood asked.

"That's what I'd like to know," Decker said. "Let's get to her apartment."

"You don't think—?"

"Let's just get there!"

They reached Linda's building in record time, and Decker was out of the cab before it had stopped moving.

"Decker!" Rosewood shouted. He was afraid Decker would charge into Linda's apartment without caution. Rosewood had come to like Decker, and he didn't want to see him killed. He pulled the .32 out of his pocket and charged into the building after him.

Decker broke the lock on the front door getting in, and when he got to the second floor, he pulled the shotgun out and blew the lock off Linda's door.

"Decker!" Rosewood said, coming up behind him.

Decker held his finger to his lips and motioned for Rosewood to flatten himself against the wall.

"Either she's inside dead, or there's somebody inside waiting," Decker whispered.

"What do we do?"

"I go in," Decker said. "You stay out here until I call you."

"But I—"

"Wait here!"

The door was flapping back and forth from the force of the shotgun blast. Decker put his foot out to stop it, then slipped into the room, keeping low.

He looked right and then left, then moved farther in and checked the bedroom.

She wasn't there, and neither was anybody else. He lowered the shotgun, aware that his heart was beating extra fast. A drop of perspiration dripped from the end of his nose and landed on the toe of his boot.

"Billy!"

"What happened?" Rosewood asked, coming in, .32 in hand, shaking.

"She's not here."

"That's not one of your choices," Rosewood said.

"I know," Decker said, "and neither was that." He pointed to the bed.

"What?"

"That."

Rosewood looked closer and saw a note on the pillow. Decker went to the bed and picked up the note. It said,

DECKER,

CENTRAL PARK. MIDNIGHT.

ARMAND COLES

"He's got her," Rosewood said.

"Yes."

"Midnight—that's in fifteen minutes," Rosewood said.

"I know," Decker said. "His timing is perfect."

"What are you gonna do?"

Decker crumpled the note in his hand and said, "I'm going to be there."

Chapter Thirty-four

"The note doesn't say where in Central Park," Rosewood said on the way. Decker was sitting on top of the cab with him instead of inside.

"I'll just have to walk until he finds me."

"With that big bulls-eye on your back?"

"There's no other way."

Rosewood drove Decker to the Central Park South entrance of the park.

"Why here?" Decker asked.

"It's the closest to where we were," Rosewood said. "First entrance we'd come to."

"It's as good as any," Decker said. He dropped down to the ground and looked up at Rosewood. "Get lost, Billy."

"Sure you don't want me to come with you?"

"He's answering *my* challenge, Billy."

"Yeah, but—"

"Thanks for everything, Billy," Decker said. "Now get lost."

Decker waited until Rosewood's cab had turned down Eighth Avenue. Then he turned and walked into the park.

Inside the park, Armand Coles waited. Decker's driver had taken him to the Bucket of Blood. That meant he knew the city. When Decker told him Central Park, Coles figured the driver would take him to the nearest entrance.

Now he watched Decker walk into the park and followed him a way—Decker on the path, Coles through the trees and brush. It would be easy to pick Decker off from here, but that wouldn't be accepting the challenge.

Would it?

Decker heard Coles.

Armand Coles had been born and raised in the city. He knew nothing about moving silently through the brush. He was making more noise than a herd of five-year-old Indian boys.

Decker knew that challenging the man, bruising his pride, would work.

He would have him.

Suddenly, Decker was gone!

Just like that, as the path curved out of Coles's view for a second, the man vanished.

Coles backtracked and tried to find him again, but it was no use. Had he changed his mind and run back out of the park? No, Coles thought, he would have heard him running.

"Damn it, Decker, where are you?" Coles yelled.

"Right here, Coles," Decker said from behind him.

Coles froze.

"How—?"

"You should learn how to move through brush, Coles," Decker said. "You picked the one place to meet in this city where you'd be at a disadvantage instead of me."

"You son of a bitch," Coles said. "You challenged me."

"And you lost," Decker said. He pressed the shotgun into the small of Coles's back and said, "Just stand still." He patted the man down and removed a Colt .45 from a shoulder rig.

"Isn't this a little uncomfortable?"

"I usually carry something small."

"This was for my benefit?"

"Yeah."

"I guess I should be flattered," Decker said. He moved back three steps and replaced the shotgun inside his coat and then switched the .45 to his right hand. "I should be, but I'm not."

"Oh, and why is that?"

"Because I'm a little tired, a lot beat up and very angry and—" He stepped forward and brought the butt of the .45 down hard on the point of Coles's shoulder.

"Oh, Jesus!" Coles shouted. Decker lifted his foot and drove the heel into the back of Coles's left knee. The man staggered and went down, holding his shoulder.

"Where's the girl?"

"Listen, Decker—"

Decker grabbed Coles's left fist, twisted it behind him and brought the .45 down on it hard. The sound of the arm breaking was sharp and loud, and Coles screamed.

"Where's the girl?"

"Jesus, my elbow—"

Decker grabbed the broken arm and pulled it back. Coles screamed again.

"You've got one broken arm, Coles," Decker said. "You want to try for two?"

"I don't know—"

Decker put the .45 next to Coles's left ear and fired it. Coles screamed.

"Jesus, I'm deaf!"

"OK," Decker said, "you got a broken left arm, a bad left knee, and you're deaf in your left ear." He grabbed Coles's right arm, pulled it straight back and said, "Let's start on the right side."

"No, wait," Coles said, gasping out the words. He was crying now. "Jesus, wait—"

"I'm not going to wait very long."

"Let me . . . let me get my breath!"

"Uh-uh," Decker said. "I let you get your breath, you might try to lie. Talk now, Coles." Decker pulled tight on the arm. "Talk, or be a cripple for life."

"OK, OK," Coles said. Decker released his arm and stepped back. In that moment, Coles reached into his boot and came out with a knife and lunged at Decker. Decker squeezed the trigger of the .45 and blew off the top of Coles's head.

"Shit!" Decker snapped.

He heard someone running, and he turned, holding the .45 out in front of him.

"Hey, wait—" Rosewood said, both hands held out in front of him. In his right hand he held the .32.

"Billy, I told you to—"

"I know, I know, get lost," Rosewood said. He looked down. Coles's left arm was lying at an odd angle, and the top of his head was missing.

"He killed himself," Decker said, sticking the .45 in his belt.

"He killed *himself*?" Rosewood said. "How?"

"With stupidity," Decker said. "Come on, let's get out of here."

When they came walking out of the park, Largo was standing there.

"Is Coles dead?" he asked.

"He's dead," Decker said.

"You've got a big rep in the West, Decker."

"Do I?"

"I been thinking about going west. It would help if I went with a rep."

"Mine?"

"I was thinking about that."

"Well, don't," Decker said. "Not tonight, Largo. I've got other things to do."

"I know."

"Do you?"

Largo nodded.

"The girl."

"Do you know where she is?"

"I know someone who does."

"Who?"

"If I tell you," Largo said, "will you meet me after? Just you and me?"

"Just you and me, Largo."

Largo studied Decker for a few moments, then nodded.

"You know that little café you been eating in?"

"Yeah. What about it?"

"Your friend Ready eats there, too."

"What?"

"Yeah," Largo said, laughing. "I'm surprised you fellas haven't run into each other."

"Is this for sure?"

"Oh, yes," Largo said. "And I'll tell you something else. He doesn't just eat there."

"What's that mean?"

"Talk to a waitress with firm calves."

"Most waitresses have firm calves."

Largo grinned, turned to walk away and said, "Not like this one."

Chapter Thirty-five

Decker stood just inside the doorway of the café and looked at both waitresses. He'd been wrong. One of them had very slender calves, but the other one—Marcy, the one who was friends with Linda—had nice firm ones.

She turned and smiled when she saw him.

"Hello," she said, approaching him. "Are you meeting Linda?"

"Linda's not available," he said.

"Oh?"

"She's with a man."

"Oh, I'm sorry—"

"His name is Ready, Oakley Ready."

"Oak—that's not possible," she said, frowning.

"Why not?"

"Well he's—I mean, he and I—He can't be with Linda—"

"Not only is he with Linda," Decker said, "he's holding Linda." He grabbed her by the shoulders.

"Marcy, he's going to kill her. Because he wants me."

"What for?"

"He had a friend of mine killed, had him shot in the back."

"That's not—"

"Don't tell me it's not possible," he said, shaking her. "Does he have a lot of money?"

"Well, yes, but—"

He noticed a bruise at the corner of her mouth.

"He hit you, didn't he?"

She raised her hand to the bruise.

"Look, Marcy," he said, in a gentler tone, "he wants me to know where he is. That's why he took Linda. Now tell me, before he kills her."

She stared at his chest for a few moments, then gave him an address on Delancey Street.

"Second floor," she added. "In the back."

He ran outside and shouted the address to Rosewood.

"Do you know where that is?"

"Yep!"

"Let's get there . . . fast!"

Decker had Rosewood stop the cab down the block, and they both got down.

"Stay here!" he said.

"Decker—"

"This time I mean it, Billy!" he said sharply. "Stay here."

"All right."

Decker checked the numbers on the buildings until he found the one he wanted. He tried the door and found it open.

Ready was really waiting for him.

He pulled the .45 from his belt and went inside.

He climbed the steps to the second floor, wincing as they creaked. When he reached the landing, he walked to the back. He was about to try the door when he heard noises from above—the sounds of more than one person going up the stairs. He stopped and listened.

"Decker!" a voice called from above.

He didn't answer.

"I know you're there, Decker! I've been waiting for you." There was a moment's silence, and then the voice said, *"We've* been waiting for you."

There was another moment's silence. Then he heard her cry out in pain.

"Come on up, Decker. To the roof. We're waiting—but don't keep me waiting too long."

Decker started for the stairs, then paused and went to the apartment door. It was open, and he went in. He took a quick look around. If Ready's money was there, it was hidden. After all he had spread around trying to get Decker killed, he wondered how much the man had left.

Rosewood had told him that a lot of buildings had ladders against the side, in case of fire. Decker moved to the window and saw a metal one along the side of the building. It reached from the ground floor to the roof.

He tucked the .45 back into his belt and climbed out of the window and onto the ladder.

Then he started climbing up, hoping that Ready would be expecting him to use the stairs.

The building was three stories high. Decker had been three stories high before, but never on a ladder. He hoped that it was securely affixed to the side of the building. He would hate to fall from that height. He kept climbing—it was *so* important that he reach the roof.

Finally he could reach up and grip the roof ledge. He pulled himself up until he was standing on the top rung of the ladder. From that position he could see Ready, holding Linda tightly to him with his left hand, a gun with his right. Ready was watching for Decker to come out the door from the stairway.

Decker was holding onto the ledge with both hands. He was nervous about letting go with one hand to reach for the .45. Even if he reached it, he was a lousy shot with a handgun.

He had to get up on the roof without being seen.

Jamming the toe of his boot against the side of the brick building, Decker reached for the inside of the ledge with one hand, holding the outside of the ledge with the other. He pulled himself up and quickly moved the outer hand to the inner ledge as well. In this position he was hanging there—helpless if Ready turned around. He pulled and lifted one of his legs, getting the knee up on the ledge. As he got his leg over, Oakley Ready glanced toward him. When Ready saw him, his mouth opened, and he turned, pointing his gun at Decker.

Ready fired once, but Decker pulled hard and fell onto the roof.

"Hold it right there, Decker!"

Crouched on the roof, Decker waited for Ready to fire again.

"You are Decker, aren't you?" Ready asked.

"That's right."

"You've caused me a lot of grief."

"I'm sorry."

"Ha, I'm sure," Ready shouted. "You've kept me from getting set up in this town. After you're gone, I won't have that problem anymore."

"You've got to kill me first."

"Decker—" Linda said. Decker had the impression that she was more afraid for him than she was for herself.

He understood that.

He felt the same way.

He supposed he was in love with her.

"Take that gun out of your belt and toss it away," Ready said.

Decker took the gun out and obeyed.

"Take off your jacket."

Decker took the coat off slowly, careful to hide the shotgun inside. He could have pulled it, but Linda was too close to Ready. He put the coat down on the rooftop. The knife was in his coat pocket, but it wouldn't do him any good at this distance.

"Hold your arms away from your body and turn around," Ready said, "all the way around."

Decker turned in a complete circle, arms away from his body, so that Ready could see he was unarmed.

"All right," Ready said, "all right."

He pushed Linda away from him and said to her, "Sit on the ledge."

She did so.

"On your hands," he said, "sit on your hands." She obeyed.

"All right, Decker," Ready said, motioning with his gun. Decker noticed that it was a .45, like the one he'd taken from Coles. "Over to the edge."

"Why?"

"Because you're going off, that's why."

"I could get hurt."

Ready laughed.

"You could get dead," he said. "That's the general idea."

Decker hoped Linda wouldn't try anything, but just at that moment she did.

"Linda, no—"

Linda sprang off the roof ledge, but she was painfully slow because she'd been sitting on her hands. Ready turned as she leaped at him and fired once.

Decker reached for the coat, hoping the shotgun wouldn't get wrapped up in it. He closed his hand over it, and it came free.

Ready turned from Linda and pointed the gun at Decker. Decker came up with the shotgun, and they fired together.

Ready's shot punched into Decker's left side, took a chunk of meat with it and kept going.

Decker's blast spread out as it traveled but was still lethal enough when it hit Ready to lift him off his feet and slam him against the stairwell door.

Decker dropped the shotgun and picked up Armand Coles's .45 just in case. He needn't have bothered. Oakley Ready was dead.

The question was, how was Linda?

Chapter Thirty-six

Rosewood drove Decker from his hotel to the train station the next day. Decker, had another bandage on, this one on his left side where the bullet had dug a furrow.

"You could wait a while to travel, until you heal," Rosewood had said when he picked him up.

"No," Decker had said, "I've got to leave now."

When they reached the train station, Lieutenant Tally was there, waiting.

"Come to see me off, Lieutenant?"

"Here," Tally said, giving Decker an envelope.

"What's that?"

"That will make sure you can collect the bounty on Ready."

Decker looked down at the envelope in his hand, considered giving it back, then decided that he had earned it. He'd earned it with more blood then he'd ever lost on one hunt. Dover wouldn't mind.

And he'd lost a lot more than blood on this one.

"How is she?" Decker asked.

"She's still unconscious," Tally said, "but she's going to be all right. The bullet missed her heart."

"That's good," Decker said. He was responsible for her being shot, but at least he wasn't responsible for her being killed.

"She's going to ask for you when she wakes up, you know."

"I know."

"What do I tell her?"

Decker looked over at his train and saw that it was moving.

"Tell her . . . tell her I said goodbye."

Decker started running for the train, then turned and shouted. "Hey, whatever happened to Bookman's man Largo? I thought he wanted a piece of me before I left town?"

Tally grinned and shouted back: "I guessed he changed his mind."

INTERACT WITH DORCHESTER ONLINE!

Want to learn more about your favorite books and authors?
Want to talk with other readers that like to read the same books as you?
Want to see up-to-the-minute Dorchester news?

VISIT DORCHESTER AT:
DorchesterPub.com
Twitter.com/DorchesterPub
Facebook.com (Search Pages)

DISCUSS DORCHESTER'S NOVELS AT:
Dorchester Forums at DorchesterPub.com
GoodReads.com
LibraryThing.com
Myspace.com/books
Shelfari.com
WeRead.com

✂ ☐ **YES!**

Sign me up for the Leisure Western Book Club and send my FREE BOOKS! If I choose to stay in the club, I will pay only $14.00* each month, a savings of $9.96!

NAME: _____

ADDRESS: _____

TELEPHONE: _____

EMAIL: _____

☐ I want to pay by credit card.

☐ **VISA**   ☐ MasterCard.   ☐ DISCOVER

ACCOUNT #: _____

EXPIRATION DATE: _____

SIGNATURE: _____

Mail this page along with $2.00 shipping and handling to:
Leisure Western Book Club
PO Box 6640
Wayne, PA 19087
Or fax (must include credit card information) to:
610-995-9274

You can also sign up online at **www.dorchesterpub.com**.
*Plus $2.00 for shipping. Offer open to residents of the U.S. and Canada only.
Canadian residents please call 1-800-481-9191 for pricing information.
If under 18, a parent or guardian must sign. Terms, prices and conditions subject to change. Subscription subject to acceptance. Dorchester Publishing reserves the right to reject any order or cancel any subscription.